# THE
## *Fiery*
# WOMEN

*An Inspiring Rags to Riches Story of Two Women!*

# *Disclaimer*

This novel is entirely a work of fiction. The names, characters and incidents portrayed in it are the work of the author's imagination. Any resemblance to actual persons, living or dead, events or localities is entirely coincidental.

# THE *Fiery* WOMEN

*An Inspiring Rags to Riches Story of Two Women!*

*Authored by*

## DR. S. PADMAPRIYA

penmanbooks.com

## Penman Books

Office No. 303, Kumar House Building,
D Block, Central Market, Opp PVR Cinema,
Prashant Vihar, Delhi 110085, India
Website: www.penmanbooks.com
Email: publish@penmanbooks.com

First Published by Penman Books 2020
Copyright © Dr. S. Padmapriya 2020
All Rights Reserved.

Title: The Fiery Women
ISBN: 978-93-89024-70-8

*I dedicate this book to*

*my Family*

*and*

*Uncle Gabriel Antony*

*Other Books*
*by Dr. S. Padmapriya*

*Great Heights*
*The Glittering Galaxy*
*Galaxy*

# *Preface*

My soul is in this book.

My mother was astonished when I turned into an English poet at the age of seven. Since then, both poetry and philosophy have never left me. My myriad experiences and reading habits made me more philosophical as I grew up. Since my father was an officer of the Indian Postal services, I had seen half of India by the time I turned twenty. I had travelled far and wide; from Madras to Delhi and from Bombay to Calcutta. I grew up in India and had also lived for a few years in Bangladesh, where my father had been sent to work on deputation. Later, I began my career as a lecturer of Economics, which continued for some time. My interaction with young minds, especially those in the age group of fifteen to twenty-five helped me to understand their aspirations and their tribulations, especially related to major life decisions like choice of career and relationships.

In my twenties, I also began to realise that I had a burning desire to tell a story – a story that I believed could influence young people to make the right choices in life. It would help them to choose between spiritual and material wealth and even create a path for them to achieve both. As I grew, my novel grew with me. As my own life story taught me lessons, I found my characters shaping up in a unique way and becoming more mature and wiser; much like myself.

My enriching travels, interaction with young people along with the newer experiences of marriage, love and motherhood combined with my ever-growing passion for reading and poetry – all helped me to structure my book to make it more interesting both in terms of content and language. I found that I was giving out allegorical messages in my book without actually intending to do so.

This is the manner in which, 'The Fiery Women' has turned into a socio-psychological and allegorical literary fiction set in a quasi-historical background. The book subtly combines literary beauty with mystical messages. The storyline is based on the concept of Karma and Poetic Justice. This is the story of *'One Soul, Two Lives'*.

I wish to express my deep gratitude to my mother for encouraging me to keep writing and my father to encourage me to read more. I also thank my brother for believing in me that I had the potential to scale great heights. I thank my father's friend, Mr. Gabriel Antony for guiding me in my life. I also thank my husband and daughter for loving me so much and for their infinite services.

I take this opportunity to thank everyone, who have helped me to become, who I am!

**Dr. S. Padmapriya, PHD**
*Writer and Thinker*

# Prologue

*'There is less in man than we think of,*
*And more in God than we know of,*
*The hands of **Destiny** are long,*
*It trips us and we fall.*
*When jealous predators think us doomed,*
*He helps us rise,*
*Rise like a phoenix,*
*Above them all!*
*Don't cry when all's lost,*
*Believe in **Him**,*
*For **His Prowess** is vast.'*

*At seventeen, Preetha's poem reflected her inner beauty as well as her delightful talents. Her dark body as dark as the night sky glittered with celestial beauty as one with great goodness of mind, body and spirit. Life in various orphanages had certainly made her soul, sturdier and heart, steadier. Yet, all this was never expected....life had happened at a velocity and with a force, unexpected.*

# Contents

# SECTION

## *One*

### *The Journey*

# CHAPTER

## *One*

## *The Village of D'Salem*

*'When I watch flickering lights,*
*In distant homes,*
*From my window seat on a train,*
*Or when I watch them,*
*As I walk spiritedly under an umbrella,*
*Or in a two-,*
*Or four wheeler in a rain;*
*The great spirit of wonder,*
*Gives birth to the dawn of realisation-*
*Every human and home is different,*
*This is most evident,*
*Each of us is searching for one's **Destiny**....*

This was the poem that Preetha's elegant mind was conjuring up as she walked towards one of her friends' home. With this poem, our young protagonist had just shifted gears – she had made the transition from being a painter of colours to a painter of words!

The year was 1925. Twenty-two years later, India would become an independent nation. The people of Hindustan had already started to receive the fruits of intellectual freedom. Rabindranath Tagore, the Indian philosopher-poet had already won the Nobel Prize in Literature in 1913, inspiring a large number of fellow Indians to pick up the pen and turn into happy practitioners of metro-mania. The years between 1913 and India's freedom were the years when large numbers of Indians had begun to turn to writing to express their minds – their longings, angst and sufferings. Preetha was one of them.

Many foreign invaders had politically and economically conquered Bharat, several times only to have their own sub-consciousness invaded by the deep spirituality and cultural vibrancy of the scintillating and exquisite land. Bharat was an ancient land – a thriving home to thousands of great seers and philosophers. It was the land of the Mauryas, the Guptas, the Mughals, ancient lore, mythology and a mind-boggling number of diverse cultures.

*India had lost much of her regal splendour owing to British rule, which had replaced the ancient Indian cultural supremacy with its own. India was struggling to know her real self. Was she, the ancient Goddess or a modern one? 1947 would be the year that Mother Bharat would realise that she was still the same time-revered Goddess but in her modern independent avatar.*

Preetha's story begins in a village in British ruled India. The year was 1906. A year ago, Lord Curzon had partitioned Bengal. The name of the village was D'Salem. It was nestled far away from the hustle and bustle of crowded towns. There had been a huge uproar in the nation against the divisive imperialists. The people of the subcontinent of India were feeling very angry and rightly so. They were feeling anguished and terrorised by the evil state policy of 'divide and rule', practised by the British Government. This was a favourite policy of the British imperialistic rulers - used by them to terrorise all their conquered colonies, be it in Asia or America or elsewhere. The British imperialist rulers were known to be using every kind of human trick to deceive Indians and steal the vast wealth of India; be it spices or jewels. The rich land of India and millions of its people were exploited by the British imperialists. India had sahibs, memsahibs, dirt, the genteel, the not-so-genteel and millions of tolerant suffering Indians, who had endured incessant exploitation by the white masters for almost two centuries. Britain had exploited India to the hilt, taking away, just about everything from her including cotton, gold, the 'Kohinoor Diamond' and the 'Peacock Throne'. England practised mercantilism and lived up to its reputation as the 'land of shopkeepers'. The English rulers became richer at the expense of India. The powers, which lay with The East India Company, had now been wrested by the British Crown. For the English imperialists, India was like the legendary 'Kalpavriksha' or 'Wish-Fulfilling Tree'.

Yet nothing could satisfy the gargantuan greed of the rulers of the 'land of shopkeepers'. The English leaders and businesspersons were known for their greed and it was the greed of the English masters forced upon the Indian masses, which led to the decline of the great and ancient land of Bharat. Of course, the Indians too, were responsible to a certain extent to what was happening to them. Instead of concentrating their efforts on fighting against the greed of the British masters, they had indulged in in-infighting, greed, backstabbing etcetera. Slowly and surely, the rich Indian cultural ethos of goodness and tolerance began evaporating and started to disappear into the disturbing, gaudy and shady atmosphere created by the despairing oblivion of colonial rule. India like other countries, which had been ravaged by imperialism, faced a state of complete dissolution. India had become poor and weak as a result of British rule.

*However, before leaving the subcontinent in 1947, the imperialists gave India, a most precious gift. In the future, the gift of the English language would help generations of Indians to reach out to the entire world. It would go on to become one of the most respected and widely spoken languages of the world.*

D'Salem was situated in the southern part of British India - quite far away from the predatory eyes of the British rulers! It was as picturesque a place as a brilliant imagination could conceive. It was a hilly place where rainy days were as common as memories and dreams. It often rained so hard and for days together that during those times, the simple people of the town would not venture out much during the rains. They would become captives, in their own homes. Landslides were a constant threat here and thus, the people were incessantly bothered by the possible losses to people and property.

The heavy rains and the resultant continuous possibility of landslides were efficient deterrents. The British ruling community did not want to visit D'Salem. According to them, D'Salem was 'too insignificant'. Thus, while most parts of India were reeling under the pressures of the British rule, a few places including D'Salem escaped the radar of the preying eyes of the imperialists. People in D'Salem worked very hard and the forces of nature were feared and revered. The residents of D'Salem kept themselves busy all the time. They were almost always engaged in various agrarian tasks. Agriculture was the main occupation of the people who lived in D'Salem and persons of both genders were involved in the agrarian way of life. Here, the women worked as hard as the men on the fields (along with taking care of their home and household chores like cleaning, cooking and child-rearing) but received only half the wages that their men folk earned (and this happened even in the civilised twentieth century!). But overall, the people of D'Salem were a mostly a bunch of contented souls, where the women were respectfully treated (in most cases!) by the men folk.

It was D'Salem - the non-descript place, which gave Preetha, her identity. This was her first home. This was where she felt safe and happy. She was over seven but less than eight. Her tall and elegant frame often made other people to guess her age to being closer to ten than to seven. At the tender age of five, she was already helping out her grandmother in the performance of household chores. Her scanty experience brought with it, enormous positive thinking. She was a happy kid. She loved her grandmother even more than her parents; for they were always busy and had no time to spare for their daughter. Every day, after completing the household chores, Preetha's mother would go to work in the fields. Her contribution to their land was immense. She was an expert in both paddy and groundnut cultivation. She worked harder than most of the men in the fields and was able to earn and save more money for her family than her male colleagues (who would sometimes drink toddy and keep lying like snakes among the green fields, a real trouble!). And since, her mother was both a smart and selfless worker, the landowner often trusted her with more work and less wages!

Preetha's father was a postman. He was an honest government servant, who would discharge his duties of delivering letters judiciously. No rain, flood or landslide could ever stop him as he would zigzag his way over hills and plains. It used to be a delightful experience watching the actions of this spirited man on his mission of delivering messages. In fact, the whole village was always busy. Sometimes, Preetha had a lot of time to do anything that she liked after completing the household duties, assigned to her by her grandmother. She would then, spend her time listening to her grand-mother's stories, doing a little bit of this and that!

*Ignorance about the queerness of life provides children with natural immunity against imbalances, deficiencies, sorrows and negativity. Existence was beautiful and simple. There was no fear, no anger, no sorrow and no disgust. There was no need to display any emotion in excess.*

Preetha went about performing her little duties with faith and happiness. She would listen to the stories narrated by her grandmother. She loved her grandmother's spellbinding ways of storytelling. She would go into raptures and would feel richer than the richest children in the world. The simple and inexpressible joys of happy experiences coupled with a wonderful imagination made her feel so. Preetha was neither rich nor famous but she always felt insanely happy!

*Adults tend to seek fame and wealth but thankfully, the requirements of children are different. Then again, sometimes, some adults never seem grown up. These rare adults are like children and seek security, love, peace and happiness, above everything else. And this was the area wherein Preetha scored full marks.*

Preetha was very happy. It was a state of natural happiness with small influencing factors like paper rockets, paper boats, terracotta clay, hot samosas, kachories and other Indian savouries, mud toys, coconut water and sugarcane juice! There were almost no worries at all! It was just the rhythmic cycle of life playing out, without many mortal fears or favours. Preetha felt blissfully blessed and contended.

*She would retain a child's curiosity and characteristics throughout her adult years in spite of all the challenges and obstacles that life would throw at her. She would grow up to be a fiery woman – a woman, who would have the courage to speak The Truths and to express her thoughts, well. She would grow up to be bold and strong with a penchant for overcoming obstacles.*

Preetha loved lying on the mud, in the cold mornings and warm afternoons, with her face turned towards the occasional sun, (the flirty happy sun, playing hide and seek amongst the clouds in the azure expanses!) tilting it at appropriate times to catch the mercy of the Sun God. The Sun God would often oblige. He would invariably stand over her and she would sleep for hours, under his protection. It was a most beautiful feeling; very earthy and very real. This was the beginning of the life and times of Preetha. Preetha loved the rains, the rainbows, the sun, the sunshine, the rising and setting of the sun, the dark flora and their dark shadows on darkened wet evenings, the smell of the wet earth and in fact, everything natural and God given; free from wickedness, human chicanery and the strappings of materialism, thus enjoying the subtle beauty of every natural creation without the kind of prejudice that adults often display. For Preetha, all these natural occurrences created a deep sense of joy and her artistic mind enabled her to enjoy all that was aesthetic around her with even greater fervour. Preetha had a beautiful mind, which had created in her, an extraordinary connoisseur of beauty. She was beginning to observe the transience of life. Nothing is still. Everything moves. *Preetha was beginning to realise that everything including time and destiny keeps changing.* She always thought, 'This too, shall pass.'

This twenty-eighth day of February of 1907 felt truly beautiful to Preetha. It was just a month ago when Preetha had observed that several trees in her locality had become barren. The leaves on them had withered and fallen away. Now the trees were laden with leaves. Preetha felt blessed to have observed so closely the miraculous rejuvenating powers of nature. Till this moment in her life, Preetha had not understood the magnificent powers of nature. 'Everything in nature rises and falls. Man may fall but man can rise, too,' thought Preetha.

Time leapt and several of Preetha's playmates enrolled in school. Preetha's father, the postman of D'Salem was confident that his daughter was better off at home than at school. The postman decided that it was not necessary for his daughter to go to school. She was asked to assist her mother at home and on the agricultural lands. Preetha didn't mind this at all. At her age, she did not realize the impact that this single wrong decision would have had on her entire life. Her entire reality would take a beating because of her late schooling. In spite of the bitter fact that she was not able go to school herself, she maintained her friendship with her friends, who had started going to the village school. Her young friends obliged her by teaching her, a little bit of language and art and giving her, some of their pencils, erasers and brushes. Soon, Preetha picked up the fundamentals of language construction but her heart was more drawn to drawing and painting. Preetha began drawing pictures with her handsome instruments: pencils and paint brushes. Her understanding about the world increased with the progress in her artistic talents. Painting was Preetha's first love. It would many years later that her passion for colours would give way to a lasting passion for patterns with words. It was only later that she would realize the value of formal education, when she would get the opportunity to attend school. Since paper was a luxury for Preetha, she made up for the loss by using the village walls. Preetha was a wonderful artist and her strokes produced a kaleidoscope of colors and images on the sun-burnt cement walls. The village people were gentle folk and did not consider this blatant display of a child's artistic talents on their walls, as an irritant and were rather happy to have their walls decorated, free of cost. Every now and then, a kind person of the village would appreciate Preetha and her being would turn warm with gratitude and joy. This unadulterated experience of joy caused by genuine appreciation created confidence in the little girl to want to do more to make her people happy. Drawings and paintings were the only two gifts that she could offer and those gifts were graciously accepted by the wise villagers. With such an understanding and adoring group of fans, our little artist felt very appreciated and respected. She drew many pictures: father, mother, brother, sister, the farms, the ducks, the hens, peacocks, pigs and just about everything from her surroundings that could inspire her creativity and most importantly, which she could relate to. She used natural colours made from flowers and leaves. The green grapes yielded a yellow colour and the black berries yielded a dark violet colour, which turned brown when used on the whitewashed walls. By the time, she was past eleven; most of the village walls carried the impression of the strokes of her brush and were drenched in colour. Preetha imagined that such wondrous days would last forever. She loved the tortoise paced life of her village. The pace seemed enchantingly endless. But as is the case with all good things, the good times didn't last.

One day, there was an earthquake. It was one unlike any other and the first one in a long time in D'Salem. It was a scary experience for Preetha. The houses fell, the trees fell, the rocks tumbled, the bricks tumbled and the delightful village lake as well as the adjoining land rocked liked a cradle. However, for some inexplicable reason, some of the walls of the village, which had her artistic revelations on them, remained intact. The drawings and paintings dazzled like gems in the sun. Relief work started in full swing.

At first, Preetha did not understand the repercussions of the earthquake. For Preetha, the earthquake was a giant monster, which ate up everything which came its way. Many villagers had perished and property had been destroyed. Only a few walls in the village had resisted the impact of the earthquake. Patriots and humanists provided food and clothing in abundance. The entire nation came together and even the British administrative machinery did its best to contribute to the welfare of the injured and homeless. The good work of the British nurses and doctors during this devastating earth-quake were one of the few high points of the British rule in India.

The earthquake was an eye-opener for Preetha. Till then, she had imagined that the entire world was full of bliss and peace. For the first time, in her short years of existence did Preetha realize that the world was not all that simple and that neither relatives nor friends can be present there for an individual, at all times. It would be many years later that she would get to read about the spiritual teachings of The Lord Gautama Buddha, who said, 'No one saves us except ourselves. No one can and no one may and that neither mother, father nor any other relative can do one greater good than one's own well- directed mind. Not God, but goodness is the support of man.' From her future studies, she would be able to understand the same message given in different scriptures that one ought to lift the self by the self. This would be given in the Upanishads, the ancient Hindu scriptures containing the commentaries on the Vedas.

One would need to acquire strength of one's own by one's own hard work and sustain that strength on one's own merit throughout one's life. That would be the secret code of success in life.

When the news of the disappearance of her parents reached her, Preetha became very upset. Their house was now, mere debris. The earthquake had struck at eight in the morning and that her mother had perished was quite certain. Her mother must have been inside the kitchen.

Preetha had been playing outside on the fateful day. Her father was nowhere to be seen and it felt as if he had disappeared from the face of the earth, forever. Preetha cried and cried. Preetha thought that her uncles and aunts would be out there to support her. But she soon realized that her relatives were distancing themselves from her. They appeared to be pretty certain that the child would eat up their resources! At that tender age, it was beyond Preetha's understanding that people could be so full of the milk of human kindness and compassion! She shrank into her immaturely formed emotional shell, which was full of anger, desperation, irritation and a growing anger against all mankind. In the long trek through tricky, treacherous and timeless time, she would grow up to understand about human wickedness, ingratitude, cruelty and chicanery, the strappings of materialism and artificialism and all about vanity and diabolism. The first flame of life had engulfed her. The first and important lesson about life had entered her conscious and sub-conscious; the lesson, which taught her that not all people can be trusted. But she would also realize that dark clouds give life-sustaining cool rains. Preetha forgot her tears and swallowed her rage. She didn't want to waste her life in regret. She wanted to pick the fragments of her, which had fallen. She knew that she would have to rise each time she would fall – and on her own. The first fiery and difficult experience of life had burnt her. Preetha wanted to progress, now as a person of *fiery* spirit would!

# CHAPTER
## *Two*

## *Vreetapur Days - Life in an Orphanage*

Preetha was now an orphan with fewer resources. Someone decided that the children ought to be taken from the site of the earthquake to an orphanage in Vreetapur. It was the idea of a local leader, Abu Shakil. He was one of the more popular and well-mannered leaders of D'Salem.

Vreetapur was a town near D'Salem and the orphans of the village were taken there. Vreetapur was a beautiful town, unpolluted and serene; caressed and blessed with nature's abundance. A muddy pond and the numerous water snakes, which lived there on the orphanage's campus along with the deep green foliage, were among the first sights and smells to welcome Preetha and her companions. The children soon learnt to avoid the dangers of nature, leaving the water snakes in a state of alarm at the sudden upsurge in the intelligence levels of the former. Soon, Preetha developed a taste for the bitter-sweet fruits of the Neem tree opposite the orphanage. She began to enjoy the process of eating the bitter-sweet Neem-fruits in the manner that other people begin to like eating banana or jackfruit chips. 'The human personality is as complex as these sweet-bitter fruits. Virtue and vice often co-exist in people,' thought Preetha, as the first pearls of a rational understanding of the world found their way from her conscious mind to her subconscious mind.

Time flew at an incomprehensible speed for Preetha. Preetha would be completing twelve summers, the following monsoon. Preetha liked the fact that she could be fiery. Although the shock of the consequences of the earthquake had shattered her life, it was not sufficient to break the resilience of a fiery personality like Preetha who was proud of being both courageous and virtuous. It was a source of immense pride and joy to her that she could accomplish many things without compromising on her ethics. This was a matter of great personal satisfaction to her. After all, she would not have the privilege of having many to guide her throughout life except for a few righteous people and some good books containing the great secrets of mankind along with benevolent Nature with all its magnificence and enormity. The truth was that Preetha was her own guide just as much as other people are. 'No one can do things for us. The truth is that each individual attracts a certain kind of destiny based on what they desire and what they do. Of course, it might be one's subconscious nature carried over several births, which might be the actual factor, which molds our character,' thought Preetha.

Preetha belonged to a rare breed. Preetha was always kind to the weak or vulnerable. She was free from the tragic flaw, which afflicts most Homo sapiens – the cruel desire to exploit those, weaker than themselves! Though born a Hindu, raised now in a Christian Home for orphans - her behavior and art of living was always that of a Buddhist. Of course in matters of lifestyle, she didn't have too much of a choice. There was this hostel food with uncooked carrots and beans, unnatural looking curds, smelly plates and what not! She suffered a lot but bore her sufferings very cheerfully. She never complained, abused or turned violent and instead bore all her sufferings with stoic resilience. Without knowing anything about Buddhism, she was being the perfect Buddhist with its philosophy of leaving all evil to be burnt by its own evilness. Life situations would shake her out of her comfort zone and test the limits of her endurance. 'Maybe, my present pains would lead to great future gains,' thought our well intentioned young girl. This young girl surely did not have nerves of steel; as yet. It would take more life experiences to develop all of that.

On one Friday, towards the end of the first year of her stay in the orphanage, the Controller of the orphanage sent for Preetha. The cunning woman seemed to be looking for some information. 'Where are you from?' asked the controller in a disquieting voice. 'From D'Salem, where Venu, the postman lived,' said

Preetha. D'Salem was one of the many places, which had been affected by the killer earthquake and Preetha was one of the lucky ones, who had been able to escape to a better future. A lot of children in her village had gone missing; probably lost to dreaded child traffickers. 'He is my father. Here, there is no postman to bring us letters. I paint less now. I used to paint a lot, earlier but now I have lost interest in drawing. I think my experiences have got something to do with this change. I like to write more now. Education is a fine ornament. It has helped me to express myself. But only my ways of expression have changed. Earlier, my tools were colours. Now, I use words. I am an artist. Writing is an art just like drawing, sculpting, acting or painting or singing. This is the truth about writing. All art is to express ourselves. All contain a creative component and a message component. In my village, everyone knew how good a painter, I was. At that time, I didn't go to school and so, I didn't know to write. Now, in this school, they have taught me how to write and so I write. I like writing more now. I don't need anything except for some paper and a pen. Painting is expensive. You need brushes, colours and people's patience,' said Preetha. Preetha was as simple as a child could be. The words, which sprung from her tongue, needed neither prodding nor cajoling.

The truth was that Preetha was a wonderful child; a perfect compound of goodness, intelligence and beauty. Virtue, intelligence and beauty makes for an excellent combination beyond valuation. Preetha was this rare child in whom virtue, beauty and intelligence, sat comfortably in unison. The teachers of her school had made a great impact on her character-building.

Christian missionaries ran the school and they filled the minds of the children with thoughts of the divine. Preetha liked the school prayer, very much. There were many days, when Preetha would repeat the school prayer, in silence.

*'Just go on.*
*You need not despair,*
*Thou shall be fearless,*
*None need to kneel before evil,*
*Why kneel before sin and sinners?*
*Embrace my teachings,*
*You shall triumph.*

*Never turn away,*
*From the chosen path of virtue,*
*It revels in its revealing.'*

The prayer would calm and soothe Preetha's frightened nerves. It was like her secret tonic. Another slothful year passed filling the young child's mind with dreadful dark anxieties like the dark passages of her dull school.

One day, the Controller of the orphanage, sent for her again. As soon as the young girl entered the office room of the school, the Controller almost pounced upon Preetha. In a rather unfriendly voice, she began to speak. 'Did you say that you are from D'Salem and that you are an artist?' The controller of the orphanage was an irritating woman whose dead pan voice often reminded the children that they were orphans. The Controller of the orphanage was quite devoid of the quality of compassion. She was a pure business-woman, who cared much more for the money that the donors gave to care for the children than the children, themselves.

More than a year had passed between their earlier conversation and this one. Preetha did not harbor any negative feelings towards the Controller for her lack of compassion. She replied in the affirmative.

'A couple has come from Gilorea. They have come to see you. They saw your paintings in your village. They want to promote your art. They have come to help you to become wealthy and famous. This is a very good chance for you to display your talent. Be deferential to them and I hope that you will always be grateful to me, for introducing you to them.' At that precise moment, Preetha gazed at the giant tree in front of the orphanage. The child's mental state was as disheveled as the wizened branches of that tree.

The next day, the Gilorean couple came to meet Preetha. The Controller of the orphanage introduced Preetha to the Giloreans. 'She is one of our most talented students,' said the Controller. A fair woman with golden hair spoke. 'Are you the artist?' asked the charming woman. Preetha replied clearly. 'Yes,' she said. Her voice was steady and strong. It did not reveal the strained life of an orphan. The strength in her voice arose out of her convictions.

The name of the majestic looking woman was Cinnamona. Cinnamona began to speak. 'Your paintings are beautiful and very expressive. There is grace in your art and a sense of calm in it. The theme of your painting is rural but they have a universal feel.' Preetha accepted the appreciation with a smile - the smile of those, who have undergone unspeakable sufferings.

The next day, the couple came back to the school to meet Preetha. Preetha took her seat and sat quietly before her visitors. Cinnamona broke the silence by initiating an interesting conversation and soon, Preetha's tongue loosened.

Preetha began, 'Do you like my country?'

Cinnamona replied, 'We adore your land. It is full of cultural and spiritual insights.'

Preetha interrupted, 'Yes, it's true. It is also full of disparities. The truth is that some of my own people are highly selfish, dishonest, cruel and ungrateful. It is also true that my country ranks higher on parameters like population, pollution and corruption rather than on performance and human indices. We have few good leaders. Right now, the ones at the top are really good and this is happening after a long time. Mahatma Gandhiji, Subhash Chandra Bose, Sardar Vallabhai Patel and Nehru are really working hard to get freedom for India. They are really good people. We have no dearth of good leaders, now in Bharat. Every day, the land produces more and more brave-hearts. They come from every direction- north, south, east and west. They come from every faith and affiliation. They all have just one objective – securing independence for India. I hope the people will keep supporting them. Swami Vivekananda, the great Hindu cyclonic monk has taught that it is not just sufficient to fight again evil but also to support the good. This is India's best chance to get freedom. A fair and just society is the outcome of the interplay between good leaders and good people. It is very wrong to put all the blame on the leaders for every fallacy in a country.'

Cinnamona accepted Preetha's statement, with a slight nod of her head.

Preetha said, 'In our country, out of every amount collected as tax money, a huge portion goes towards defence expenditure and on repaying the interest on loans taken; all very unnecessary expenses, when large sections of the people are starving.'

Cinnamona said, 'You seem to know a lot.'

Preetha replied, 'We have a good tutor and she keeps us well informed. I also read the daily newspaper.'

Cinnamona said, 'I appreciate your knowledge. In our country, we pay a lot of money as tax but we also have a whole lot of services being provided for free. Health care is free.'

Preetha replied, 'I wish it was possible here. Then, people need not suffer.'

Looking at Cinnamona's companion, Preetha then asked, 'Is he your husband?' Cinnamona replied, 'We live together but he hasn't married me.'

Preetha said, 'Kindly do marry him. In our country, marriages are sacred. It is an eternal bonding; physical and spiritual. We don't believe in live-in-relationships.'

A moved Cinnamona said nothing but thought, 'How wise, this child is! Age does not seem to have much correlation with wisdom.'

It was around eleven in the morning when the couple returned to the orphanage. Their faces shone with a strange light. The shiny ring on Cinnamona's face confirmed what Preetha's intuition is told her. Preetha felt happy that the couple had taken the sacred wedding vows. The Giloreans began the conversation. They asked Preetha to express her views about her country. The conversation turned out to be an eye opener for the Giloreans. Cinnamona said, 'Listen, whatever you have spoken so far, has helped us to expand our knowledge about this country. It is your unaffected views, which has captivated us. You speak from your heart. Your views are new and profound. We are grateful to you and want to help you in some way. We will create an account in your name and we will send you some money, every month. It will act as a security for you, as you grow up and will come to your aid, when you will want to pursue higher education.' Preetha accepted their offer with gratitude.

After a few weeks, the Giloreans left the country. They did not leave without making the promise of returning back to meet Preetha. Preetha did not cry much on the day the Giloreans took the flight back to their home town. It was yet another moment of separation for Preetha. She bore the separation with patient strength for she had, by now, known about life's transience and she knew that all the promises, which were made, could not be kept all the time. 'This, too, shall pass' she said to herself. There was a God deep within Preetha's heart and she knew that this God was present in every one. This God was not any external God whom people worshipped. It was not Ram or Allah or Jesus or any God people knew by a name. This God was the voice of goodness and rationality, common to all religions. 'And then, can God really have a name? God is inexplicable, nameless, faceless, omnipotent, omnipresent and omniscient. God is in everything. God is everything. God and all creation is the same. So, everything and everyone is God. God is Goodness. God is compassion,' thought Preetha.

Soon, the Giloreans started sponsoring Preetha's education. This continued for a year. One day, the man in charge of the orphanage decided that the funds reaching the orphanage ought to be diverted through him. He changed the rules to comply with his evil intentions. When the sponsors realized the man's designs, they stopped sponsoring the education of the orphan children and Preetha became an orphan for the second time.

The future appeared full of mystery and suspense for Preetha. But she was not afraid. She had learnt to be patient in unpredictable situations. She was learning to cope with change. 'Nothing is permanent. Who knows about anything? Nobody knows about anything in totality. Life is but a sum of assumptions, beliefs, thoughts, memories, interpretations and dreams. The mysteries of life have always fascinated man and tantalized him. He lives in this unbreakable bubble where one sequence of events merges with the next to form a pleasant or unpleasant lineage. He raises his mighty fist to change the course of his life but the roller coaster in which he rides, is too fast paced to allow him to get down. A human being has got no knowledge of where he is heading and he realizes that he can get down only at the end of the trip; and even the destination is not left to his choice. The heart desires to attain great heights and nice dreams are meant to be fulfilled. The dot, the distance, the diametric and the divide exist everywhere. The final winner is the one who retains the strength to withstand the pressures of life till the end,' thought Preetha. When Preetha was told that her sponsors had stopped sending funds to her account, she was not disheartened. She was now older than before and age had brought with it, a certain level of maturity. It had brought with it, a certain realization that the path to success is full of adversities and that one would have to necessarily, cling on to single strands of wisdom and hope to realize success, truth and stability in any endeavor and in the most important of all endeavors; life, itself.

# CHAPTER

## *Three*

## The 'Green City'

*The mind is a distraught being. It searches in futile what lies before it and it searches and analyses what it might never face. It is swallowed by the past and is engrossed by what might happen in the future. It forgets that there is a present to be lived. Yet, the joy in life would be lost if the mind forgets the past, for then, all the beautiful feelings, sights, tastes, smells and sounds would be lost forever and we would not be blessed with the chance to redress, the mistakes of the past and hope for a better future. Without a future, life would not be worth living for. This is a world, where changes are rapid, be it in the world of emotions, of matter or of energy. Man was born to live in peace and with virtue, by God like the rest of the creations of God but he, with his intelligence has managed to create wonders, vice and violence. In a virtuous world, there would be no conflicts and no courts, lawyers, police or judges, no patients and no doctors, no crime and no sorrow. But then people don't like being in a perfect world.*

Preetha was as much a prisoner of her past and future like all her friends. She was full of insecurity because of the uncertainty that lay ahead. She wanted to continue on the path of virtue but she was also sure that life would throw up many obstacles and troubles to test her patience and resilience. She would have to overcome an endless stream of obstacles and opponents. She wanted to keep fighting against all forms of evil but there was no way to know if she would always be successful against them. The future is always in the future. Preetha decided to keep trying to remain good and successful. 'At least, let me keep trying. There is always a possibility of success as long as you don't give up,' she thought.

Preetha and her orphan friends completed their primary education at the orphanage in Vreetapur. However, there were no facilities for higher secondary education in the same place. The government of the country ordered that the surviving children of the earthquake be provided with good education in a school especially created for the surviving children of the deadly earthquake. The destitute children from D'Salem were to be taken to the Green city. They were to go there by the 'Vichitram' Express, an express train starting one stop before D'Salem.

The train started on time. It was the month of August and cool winds had started blowing. The weather was quite magical with streaming and pouring buckets of sunlight. The afternoons were hot and the evenings were appeased by mild drizzles. It was as if there was some silent understanding amongst the Sun God, the Wind God and the Rain God. Surprisingly on the day of departure, it was very windy and the orphan children had to wear their scarves very tightly over their heads.

The children climbed on to the train, gossiping all the while about what they would find in the Green City. The Green City was so called because of its greenery. Soon, the children started chattering incessantly about various things such as the length of their train, the deep gorges on the way, the streams, the rivers and the mountains. The orphans had not travelled much outside their own little world and so this was like an outing for them. Each child felt a sense of profound freedom. When one is young, sorrow is easily forgotten and the world becomes vast and unending. Children know no jealousy or conspiracy. They do not know about the great deal of evil, which exists in the world. They do not know about the disparities of life. They know very little about exploitation, jealousy, anger, lust or hatred. Ignorance being bliss, knowledge is sometimes the enemy.

But Preetha was a different child. She looked around to examine her co- travelers in her compartment. Her eyes scanned the different people, present in all sizes and shapes and from different backgrounds but whose immediate destination was common; the 'Green City'. Her eyes settled on a gruff looking man sitting near her, on the opposite side near the window. A young girl child of around six years accompanied him. They didn't appear to be relatives or father-daughter. Every now and then, the elder of the two spoke to the little one in a quiet but tough tone. It was quite clear to the co-passengers that the young child was scared but no one dared to get up from their seats and reach out to her. Preetha overheard their conversation.

The man was saying, 'Keep quiet. Don't make a sound. We will get down at Bandarpur. You are to stay with me, now.'

The girl said, 'Will you take me to the fair?'

The man said, 'Oh! Yes. You are really expensive to maintain. I have already paid twenty-five riahs to buy you from your parents.'

Preetha knew that something really evil was happening around her and she wanted to do something but what could she do? She felt helpless and troubled. Preetha thought of informing her teachers but then decided against it. Maybe they would not believe her. Maybe they would even laugh at her. *Many a time, we fail in life merely because we don't have the guts to voice our honest opinions.* Preetha was young child. She did not know how to respond to such difficult situations. Life in her village seemed much simpler than the complex characters living in the city. *She could be forgiven for not knowing how to react and confront her circumstances but what about all the adults around her? Why did they not have the guts to question the evil?*

Preetha would learn all about child abuse and human trafficking, much later. *The extent of human greed and lust is unfathomable and despicable.* She would do her bit to save the world. Preetha knew that she would have to create the world that she wanted and that no one else could do it for her. She would learn later that if she dreamt sincerely and well enough, she would realize her dreams.

The lady accompanying the children was their designated guide. She was going to be one of the teachers for the children in the 'Green city'. Her name was Mrs. Rosa. Their guide taught the following prayer to the children.

*'A holy man said,*

*'In the holy books,*

*I have read,*

*The image of God,*

*Is held.'*

*The wiser, holier man said,*

*'The sins of man cannot,*

*Be washed away by water,*

*Should not be allowed to recur or occur;*

*His presence is here,*

*There, everywhere,*

*He lives in freeness;*

*God is not owned by man,*

*Man is owned by God.'*

The train, which would decide their future, bellowed smoke throughout its route to the 'Green City'. It moved slowly with its great bellows of smoke, polluting the flora and fauna around. The train passed through the lush green forests, valleys and tunnels. Whenever the train passed through tunnels, the children squealed in delight. They had reserved their strength to scream in every dark tunnel. It was a most exhilarating experience for them. This was a memory that they would cherish for long. The train passed by Peepal trees, Ashoka trees, Mango trees, bushes, grass and fields. Some fields were lying fallow. Some other fields were being ploughed or weeded. Some fields had matured to the harvest stage. The scene reminded Preetha of her native village. At Junoor, the train stopped for a while. Everyone had breakfast at the Junoor station. The train started again. 'Man, for all his knowledge has not been able to decipher the secrets of nature,' thought Preetha. Suddenly, the skies opened up and it began to rain heavily. It rained and rained so hard that it appeared as though the mighty skies were terribly angry with something. It was quite unexpected. 'Was mother earth crying over the fate of these children in her womb or was she entertaining them to make them to forget their sorrow?' wondered little Preetha. The train arrived at the Green city and a new life began for Preetha, a life with which we will become very familiar, the life in the school in Green City. A new life of learning began for the children.

Experiences had created Preetha, just like everyone else. Her character and her sense of perspective about the world changed as she realized that all kinds of people lived in her world. She wondered if it could not be possible for the whole world to be governed by one a system, which would really care about all the people of the world and where leaders would show parental concern for men, women and children so that they could live in peace and harmony with each other. In such a world, there would be no conflicts and no diseases. 'Could such a world be possible? Could people really transform into angels?' wondered the God-fearing child. Preetha prayed to the great Gods to bless her with at least one good friend in her new surroundings to provide her with love at all times and with support, whenever needed. Nala was to become her best friend in the Green City School but Preetha did not know this, then.

In the train journey from D'Salem to the Green city, we learnt about what took place in one compartment. It will be interesting and of benefit to follow the wordy duels in the next compartment as well. In the adjoining compartment, two young college students were arguing. The topic of discussion or rather argumentation was 'corruption'. The two youngsters were in the final year of college. They were law- students at the prestigious Yade Law University. They were on the verge of graduation, the whole world appeared exciting and engaging to the young lads.

The man in the yellow shirt was Narayana and the man in the red shirt was Prithvi. Narayana was speaking very softly and clearly. There was no malice in him. He came from a good background; his parents were senior government servants, extremely upright and ethical.

They were also reasonably well-educated and well to-do; though they were never too rich. Prithvi's father was a businessman and Prithvi had been brought up in the very wicked world of business; a world filled with lies and hypocrisy and where money was 'God' and 'Greed' was its temple. *Naturally, his mind was not tuned to listen to the truths of life.*

Corruption was a big problem in their days and almost every capable youngster wanted to have a say on the disturbing problem.

Prithvi was heard saying, 'A person becomes corrupt by circumstances alone.'

Narayana said, 'A person's character is both because of circumstances and choices.'

On the opposite side, facing the youngsters sat a fat man and his pretty wife. The rotund and fashionable lady with her palm-sized handbag (which appeared as a contrast to her largeness) and her husband made a very interesting combination. The fat man was leaning forward, keenly listening to the argument between the two young men. He did not want, however, to be caught overhearing. So, he pretended to be deeply engrossed in a cinema magazine.

Prithvi asked, 'How? Can you offer an explanation?' He obviously wanted to put his friend (or was he, his enemy?) in discomfort. Narayana replied. 'There are two types of corrupt people. There are those who become corrupt by choice and those who become corrupt by circumstances. Let us first take the case of those who become corrupt by choice. They are corrupt because they want to be corrupt. We can mutually agree on the point that a person's character is determined by both nature and nurture. We cannot change our genes easily but we can change an individual by changing the way, he is brought up. Molding a child is done at school, at home and by the environment. It is a pity that schools teach children, the same old subjects like English, Maths, Science, Social science, Physics, Chemistry and biology but none teach about honesty, hard work, generosity, gratefulness and chastity. Incorporating moral science classes in schools would be an ideal thing to do. This will have a good effect on students, who will go on to be the country's next generation. This will attack corruption at the psychological level. Now, let me move on to the latter case. We have minimum wage laws. We have a planned economy. All this is excellent but much remains to be accomplished, Today, what we are having is maximum price disparity and great wage disparity. By the term, price disparity, I mean the difference in the price level of any particular commodity. In our country, this price difference is maximum. On one hand, we have a cup of tea, being sold for three rupees at the roadside shop and the same tea with a slight difference in quality is sold for two hundred rupees in a five star hotel. Some wise men attribute it to the difference in quality. It is not only due to the difference in quality but also due to the exploitation of man by man. Every individual is a victim of price disparity. It is this maximum price disparity, which drives people to resort to hook or crook to attain the higher standard of living. All desire to attain this higher end. If the government can interfere to minimize this price difference, people would lose interest in money because they would be in a position to easily satisfy their desires. A minimum price disparity is what is needed to sustain the economy, not a maximum one. Likewise, we must have a fixed maximum and minimum wage. There must be parity in the wage structure within every organization as well as between the public and private sector. The world will be truly free from corruption when people start respecting others for what they are and not for what they have.' The elderly man, who had been hearing the arguments from both sides like a silent judge, stretched his short legs involuntarily and touched the floor of the train and he got up and said, 'Bravo, an excellent argument, indeed!' Prithvi was angry with the fat man, for supporting his opponent but he maintained silence. 'I will show Narayana, who I am,' said Prithvi in a low tone to himself. Prithvi was feeling agitated but did not show it. The duo got down on reaching their destination and took an auto to their hostel.

# CHAPTER

## *Four*

# *Education and Friendships*

September was going to be a rather lucky month for Preetha. It was going to bring the bright flower of a loving friendship into her life.

Nala was a day-scholar hailing from Bada Ghar, a village near Preetha's school. Her parents were in a prison in the neighbouring country of Dilchistan. They had been taken into custody for illegally entering Dilchistan (without passports) to sell their carpets. Her grandmother couldn't find a better school than the 'Green City' school to send her grand-daughter. Preetha and Nala became classmates in the 'Green City' school. The first few days were spent in courtesies and information exchanges amongst the students. Then as in the case of some relationships, which get personal after a point of time, Nala and Preetha started to move towards a more enduring kind of relationship; the relationship of friendship. It all began on a friendly Thursday.

Preetha had been going around the large and lonely-looking school building. She had been going around the place in circles. This was a new place and Preetha was busy discovering the new nooks and corners. Her mental *global positioning system* was learning on the job. Presently, she found herself peeping into the last classroom on the second floor's badly-lit school corridor to try to seek help on how to get back to her own class. A statuesque girl came out of the room and began talking to Preetha. Quite soon, Preetha found herself speaking freely with this new girl, revealing facets of her personality and life to this new person, whom she had never seen before. Soon, Nala guided Preetha to her own class room. It would be the beginning of an enduring soul-mate friendship. The orphan girl found the warmth of a loving mother in Nala. Theirs was a friendship based on empathy and mutual respect.

Now, every month, kind donors deposited a certain sum of money into the savings account of every student in their school. Most of this money went towards the purchase of books. A large number of books were made available to the students. The school lessons were heavy and there were many exams to write, intermittently. It was exhausting for the students who often felt like car parts on the assembly line. However, Preetha did not drown in the sea of knowledge-feeding and instead, managed to retain a certain depth of a long-term vision without compromising on the abilities of the intellect. Her ability to swing from periods of great intellectual aggrandizements (benefitting from the wonderful repository of knowledge in the large quantum of books in the school library), to periods of complete non-learning was what kept her going. *Preetha had no friends or Godfather to help her. She could only look up to God to help her. Sometimes, self-motivation is the best motivation.*

Several years passed by. Time had run like a gazelle. Preetha had grown into a beautiful and wise woman. Eighteen summers had circled over Preetha and left and she had not even noticed them clearly. Preetha envisioned that God would create conducive circumstances, which would help her to blossom as an independent and successful human being. It was only much later that she would begin to realize that all that one becomes has to be attained through painstaking hard work, patience, perseverance and courage. There would be no easy way out.

She had accumulated sufficient funds to join college. The admission process in the wide world was menacing and scandalous. Being an orphan, she had to fend for herself. Finally, after a great deal of trouble, her admission process was complete and she became a full time scholar in a good college. Initially, Preetha felt wary of her new classmates. It took her some time to adjust to her new surroundings. This was her first proper 'school'. Preetha soon began to mentally distance herself from her past. The vivaciousness of the present and the sense of security that her classmates enjoyed made her take a long and hard look at her past. She knew that she would have to work harder to come to their level both in terms of general understanding of the academic subjects and also in terms of confidence levels. With the gradual progression of time, she was able to build a new bridge of friendship with her classmates. During one of her fortunate days in college, Preetha became acquainted with Kasturi, a brilliant girl. It was quite natural for them to become friends. Preetha's soft nature somehow blended with Kasturi's toughness and stubbornness. Kasturi was primus inter-pares in their relationship. They talked a lot and held views, often not in tandem with each other. They both believed in the spirit of cooperation and not compromise.

One day, Preetha told Kasturi about the little child who had been trafficked in her train during the trip to the Green City and for whom she had not been able to do anything. From the minute, Preetha told Kasturi about the incident, Kasturi began to hate men. Kasturi started to think that all the problems in the world were because of the menfolk of the world.

'Ah, the world would have been a better place without men,' said Kasturi to anyone willing to hear her. She became a staunch hater of men and decided not to marry. Kasturi was strong, bold and seemed incapable of committing any fault. Kasturi represented the ideal woman; the symbol of strength and dignity. Preetha felt very honoured to be in her company. The two teamed up for competitions and almost always won; beating their competitors with new strategies. Victory became a common occurrence for the two friends. Kasturi's strength and Preetha's knowledge made a worthy combination and the two remained unbeatable. Everyone was jealous of their friendship and tried all kinds of tricks to separate the two but they did not succeed. Such was the strength of their relationship; an undying bond of friendship and fraternity. Yet, there was going to be someone, who would come between them.

Meanwhile, the country was seeing a rise in crime rates, rapes, murders, prostitution and illegal trafficking of women. Kasturi set up her own centre of research and rehabilitation to help women caught up in such adverse circumstances. She went place to place seeking information on the subject. Kasturi provided former prostitutes with sewing machines, books and stationery. Kasturi had a vision of creating self- employment opportunities for distressed women. Kasturi had enemies in all those who had profited by the earlier unlawful regime, including pimps, brothel owners and the mafia. There was a lot of dirty politics, which was played with huge doses of jealousy, conspiracies and backbiting. The pimps hated Kasturi for interfering in their work and were on the constant lookout for a suitable opportunity to throttle her good work, bring her a bad name and if possible have her killed. Her enemies faced one disappointment after another, for Kasturi was an unusual person with unusual ways of responding to evil.

With donations pouring into her voluntary organization, Kasturi established more rehabilitation centres. Kasturi loved her work because the reward was extraordinary in terms of mental peace and satisfaction. She believed in the philosophy, 'If I do well to someone, then that someone will do well for someone else.' Due to her continuous efforts, the government began framing new laws to protect women from sexual abuse.

Even after completing her collegiate studies, Preetha kept reminding herself about the importance of learning and continued to read a lot of books. This intense desire of learning helped her to expand her knowledge base. At the same time, she tried to acquire as much knowledge as she could by interacting with intellectuals and the learned. Having completed collegiate education, Preetha decided to live independently. She left the confines of her hostel. She began to take tutorial classes for young students at her new residence,' - Door No-96, Behram Street, Green City'. She paid a rent of over 100 riahs for the residence. She taught well and the number of her students kept increasing. She taught in the morning, in the afternoon and in the evening. She was willing to teach at night but the children would not come. Soon, the bad hotel food and the heavy workload started to affect her health. The workaholic in Preetha was not permitting her to settle down. Out of every month's earning, Preetha deposited a certain amount in the bank. It was not a pleasurable experience for Preetha, who hated the long wait in the queue at bank counters to perform rigorous and often unwanted repetitive procedures. This was pre-independent India and much before sweeping post-independent India's bank reforms over a long period of time and advances in technology, which would bring banks into the homes of customers through internet banking and mobile banking. The pay-in-slip credited stress in her, the demand draft demanded patience, and the cheques caused confusion and the bank employees behaved as though the money that they were handling was their money. Back home, too, Preetha knew no peace. Preetha's landlord was a hard-hearted human, who derived pleasure in harassing his tenants and Preetha had to work hard in order to meet both ends meet. She kept writing more and more. The following poem was one of the many ensuing ones, which began to flow in desperation from her voluble pen.

*In her '**Song of Hope**', she wrote,*
*Hither there shall be no reason,*
*For grievance,*
*Today and every day,*
*In every season.*

*In the Era of Hope,*
*Every man will consider the other,*
*As his brother,*
*And the two will take steps together.*

*The rays of sun-lit hope,*
*Will be brighter,*
*When there is no terror,*
*Every heart will be kinder.*

*In the Era of Hope,*
*Women will be treated with honour,*
*Not as objects of pleasure,*
*This is not my last word yet,*
*I say this without fear.*

# CHAPTER

## *Five*

## *An Unlikely Friendship*

Time passed and several worries began to surface in Preetha's mind. In spite of her own poverty, Preetha was always generous to those poorer than herself. She could always be seen giving alms to beggars around Behram Street. Anyone would have easily mistaken her to be a rich person but she was not.

One day, when Preetha reached home, she found a letter pressed under the front door. The letter was from a certain Mr. Victor. The only 'Victor' that Preetha had heard of, was Victor, the ruling youth icon and the toast of the movie industry. 'Why has he sent a letter to me?' wondered Preetha. She opened the letter and read the contents of the letter. It read as follows:

*'Respected Madam, I want to meet you. Due to security reasons, I am unable to make a trip to your residence (I request you to forgive me for that!) but I will be delighted to receive you in my quarters. Kindly oblige. I will send my limousine at eight, tomorrow*

*morning and my manager will escort you to my residence. Thanking you. Your fan, Victor.'*

Preetha did not trust the letter. 'A letter from Victor? This must be some hoax. Why has he written such a letter to me? Surely, there must be some mistake,' thought Preetha.

The next day, around afternoon, Preetha had an unexpected guest.

'Madam, why didn't you come?' asked Victor. Preetha replied, 'Why should I? I don't know you...' She continued after a long pause. 'Well, I didn't trust the letter.'

Victor replied, 'I wouldn't have cheated you for anything in the world.'

Preetha was stupefied. She was an unknown person with no connections with the high and the mighty. It was surprising to her that the top actor of 'Woody Wood' would be claiming so much allegiance to her! 'Why has he come to meet me and what on earth does he want?' was the first thought, which entered her mind.

Mr. Victor said, 'Madam, I read your poem, 'Character Is Destiny' in the 'Sun' daily. I am highly impressed by it. I guessed that the poem-story had been written by a very special broad-minded person. Here you were exposing the deficiencies of a system going haywire. It gave me an impetus to live at a time when I just wanted to die. It is such a remarkable poem.

### 'Character is destiny'

*He is great,*
*The real man, the immortal man,*
*Who stands up for truth,*
*Even in the midst of brutes.*
*Who stands up as a beacon of benevolence,*
*Even when all around him,*
*There is violence.*
*Who believes in the immortality of justice,*
*Even when he is bulldozed under an edifice.*
*Who practices non-violence,*
*Even when pelted with a volley of violence.*
*Who is honest,*
*Even in the midst of humbling poverty,*
*Caring not for the taunting by few or majority.*
*Who struggles determinedly, works hard,*
*Even when he remains unheard.*
*Who is generous,*
*But not to a fault.*
*Who is magnanimous,*
*Who returns good for evil.*
*Who is full of gratitude,*
*Even in the midst of ineptitude.*
*Who is chaste,*
*Not succumbing to temptations, infinite.*
*Who unceasingly improves himself,*
*With no more desire than to outshine himself.*

> *Who sympathizes,*
> *Expecting no sympathy,*
> *Who helps and is kind,*
> *Truly a gem of the rarest kind,*
> *Who is punctual,*
> *Unmindful that life is a process, eventual,*
> *Who is learned, polite,*
> *Refined, cultured, sagacious, noble, erudite,*
> *He is the real human, the Immortal human,*
> *Transcending all heights.'*

Victor continued. 'There seems to be some strange powers within you, which seems to be flowing to the reader through your works. I felt strange visions enter me, when I read your beautiful poem, '*The Legacy of a Victor*'. Victor took out a poetry magazine from a bag, which he had brought with him and began reading. He began reading the poem, **'The Legacy of a Victor'**.

> *What can be a victor's legacy,*
> *Except for his victories?*
> *He who,*
> *Converts fantasy into reality.*
> *A victor's life,*
> *Tells us that life is like a sweet cup of tea,*
> *Sweet, strong, all encompassing,*
> *Joys dwell,*
> *Wherein the mind is free.'*

Soon, Preetha and Victor were engaged in a long and interesting conversation. At the end of that conversation on that fateful evening, Preetha said. 'Victor! Repeat this prayer with me.' Both began to pray together to God and aloud. Her guest had come to the right place at the right time. The prayer filled Victor's heart with great peace. For the first time in his life, Victor felt happy that he had been able to create a durable friendship with a noble human being like Preetha.

> *'I pray to the God,*
> *Who on our emotions lords,*
> *For the world to become,*
> *In totality one,*
> *Whose voice in union,*
> *Is mellifluous,*
> *Producing an impact, tremendous,*
> *Where there is freedom,*
> *From fear, from jealousy,*
> *To protect us from words angry,*
> *From within and out;*
> *I pray to the God,*
> *Who on our actions lords,*
> *For men to become,*
> *One with thee;*
> *For thoughts and mannerisms,*
> *To be healthy,*
> *And actions, which would not,*

*Make one guilty,*
*To practice, charity and chastity,*
*Emboldened by a dose of honesty,*
*And a heart filled with sincerity.*
*I pray to the God,*
*Who on our reactions lords,*
*To return a favour with another,*
*To remember a help,*
*With gratitude forever.'*

Their unified voice was mellifluous and it did produce an impact, tremendous. Preetha then spoke. 'Victor, why did you want to die? Death is not an end to life. It is only the entry to the next one. The beauty of life is in living and in wanting to live. Suicide is no answer to any of our problems. Neither suicide nor intoxication can provide us an answer to any of our problems. Only cowards resort to either of them. Rather, it gives only a bad name to the doer, as someone who did not have the guts to live.' Mr. Victor replied, thus. 'I am fed up of life and I harbour no desire to live. All my money and fame have not been able to bring me peace of mind. I am completely disillusioned with life and my mind feels bombed with conflicting thoughts.' Preetha said, 'You are young, dynamic, famous and rich. What else do you want?'

Mr. Victor said, 'Peace of mind. There is a lot of exploitation taking place in my field of work. We are forced to compromise on ethics and morality. I am a prisoner of my circumstances. To put it simply, I am a prisoner of all that's happening around me.'

Mr. Victor continued, 'I was a dropout and I was jobless. I was pushed in to this field of cinema. My parents had a lot of debts to pay off. So, they made me their slaughter-goat.' Preetha said, 'It was one Gandhi, who got freedom for India. 300 million Indians looked up to him for guidance. Do you know why he could achieve so much? He won because of his moral force and complete faith as well as commitment. The sterling moral qualities of the Mahatma made him an inspiring figure. It was one Abraham Lincoln, who emancipated the slaves in America. It took one Victor Hugo and one Dickens to open the eyes of readers towards the condition of the miserable and downtrodden. It took one Subhash Chandra Bose to make the people of India realize the power of sacrifice and selflessness. It took one Marx to bring to the collective understanding of the world, the rights of the working class. It took one Lenin to rise against the then existing malefic feudalistic society in Russia. It took one Valmiki to write the Ramayana, an epic on virtue and dignity. One person can create a world. You can accomplish anything. You can choose good roles and silently influence people around you. Look, Victor, there are two ways of coping with adverse circumstances. The first method would be to allow yourself to be decimated by the difficult circumstances. The other way would be to show courage and solemnity and stand up against injustice. The probability of success or failure in the latter situation is equal but at least, whatever will be the outcome, you will have the satisfaction of having tried.'

Preetha then placed her hands on her hips and raised her voice to make it a bit more authoritative. 'Be bold, Victor. The Victor is always the one who is victorious,' she said. Mr. Victor smiled at her courage bordering on what seemed almost childish faith and yet, there was something in her that made him want to listen to her, more and more. He felt a strong but non-romantic attraction towards her. He had this inexplicable desire to be a part of her surroundings. Whosoever came in touch with Preetha always felt this deep sense of bliss and peace. Victor felt as if he were in his Guru's presence, whenever he was with Preetha.

Their meetings became more and more frequent. One day, Mr. Victor said, 'Preetha, you are very knowledgeable. You are my Guru and sister.'

In her mind, Preetha was thrilled with the way things were turning out. She recalled with pleasure, her two poems, which had made her incredibly famous.

She then recalled the lines from her poem, 'God's Love'. How daintily, exquisite language had poured from the nib of her Parker ink pen!

**'God's love will never fail**,

*Whatever be the weather,*

*We can trust God and set sail,*

*In the deepest and most perilous of seas,*

*Even when our ship is caught up in a gale.*

*He doth not lay conditions to distribute his love,*

*He belongs to those who long for him,*
*The faithful,*
*Who have their trust upon his prowess?*
*He is the ever loving father,*
*Is virtue and kindness, a brother,*
*He doth not bother about thy skin's colour,*
*He doth not bother about thy gender,*
*He doth not bother about thy allegiance,*
*To any ideology,*
*He loves everyone for what they are individually,*
*He doth not ask for you region, religion,*
*He doth not care for your caste or creed,*
*As thou proceeds on thy lonely journey,*
*With its unknown future,*
*Look ahead with fortitude,*
*His gentleness is thy prop,*
*Goodness is God.'*

Preetha's mind recalled the poem, 'My Inner call'.

*'My door bell has been ringing,*
*I know not its author,*
*I realize that I must respond to the call,*
*The hand that rings the bell is not shifting.*
*It tells me,*
*To work continuously,*
*It tells me,*
*To work willingly,*

*It tells me,*
*To work painstakingly,*
*It reminds me,*
*To work happily,*
*It reminds me,*
*To work with sincerity,*
*It reminds me,*
*To work lovingly.*


*'Make innovations,*
*Make inventions,*
*Bring to the people,*
*New sensations,*
*Bathe the world with the goodness shower,*
*Enter the realm of emotions with power,*
*Enchant the world with mellifluousness,*
*Emboss the world with sweetness.'*

Preetha fell into a reverie.... Meanwhile, the media was agog with excitement. Journalists began spreading all kinds of mischievous lies regarding the relationship between Victor and Preetha through their gossip columns. They delightfully indulged in all sorts of mudslinging against the duo without being aware of the ground realities. Mr. Victor didn't care about his own image being tarnished but being wrongly linked to someone, who was like a sister to him was unreasonable. On one occasion, he lost his cool and verbally abused a journalist, which landed himself in trouble. The angry journalist wrote more lies in the gossip columns about Victor. When Preetha came to know about what had happened she went to the journalist and said in a hush-hush voice, 'How much will you pay me to know about my relationship with Victor?'

The journalist, Hriday replied, 'Would twenty-five thousand be sufficient for you?'

Preetha said, 'Oh! Sure!'

Hriday thought, 'This is going to make news.'

Preetha said, 'Yes, indeed. My relationship with him is the same relationship that I share with you or for that matter, with any other man in this world. I treat him like my brother.'

*Preetha's words filled with truth hit Hriday like a volcano, which erupts all of a sudden. After all, even journalists are humans! Whatever news, Hriday might have wanted to publish, we will never know. He stopped lying in his columns. In fact, he stopped writing columns altogether.*

Preetha thought, 'We are all prisoners in our body. We are all affected by the feelings of misunderstanding, jealousy, lust and anger. We create problems for ourselves and then console ourselves by saying that sorrow and joy co-exist. The real truth is that having unnecessary problems is not normal, for God created man to live in peace and joy, free from problems like the rest of his creations but we have bludgeoned every right concept.'

The next day, Preetha went to meet Victor. Preetha then told Victor, 'My dear brother, Victor - the conflicts within and conflicts with the outer world is normal. What the conscience says is final and the words of the world cannot stifle it. Why bother ourselves with the comments of the world?' Then as she relaxed on the maroon coloured sofa in the living room of Victor's home, Preetha opened up. 'Listen, I have written a poem, just for you, Victor', said Preetha writing imaginary lines with her fingers, on the sofa. The title of her poem was 'Victory'.

*'There is no greater power,*
*Than the power of your conscience,*
*No greater strength,*
*Than the strength of your will,*
*No greater wealth,*
*Than the wealth of your courage,*
*No greater virtue,*
*Than the virtue of your chastity,*
*No greater control,*
*Than the control of your anger,*
*No greater truth,*
*Than the truth of your love,*
*No greater ambition,*
*Than that of an honourable life,*
*If haven't compromised on thy power,*
*Thy strength, thy wealth, thy virtue,*

> *Thy control, thy truth, thy ambition,*
> *Victory is thine,*
> *The bell are ringing,*
> *Ringing that you have won.'*

Victor smiled again in response.

# CHAPTER

## *Six*

## *Nala*

Nala was in for a great emotional upheaval. Nala's father and mother who had crossed the international border illegally to enter the neighbouring country and for which, the two had been lodged in different prisons there for the past many years, were now getting released. Nala, who was staying with her maternal grandmother, was excited. After all, Nala had been living like an orphan, notwithstanding the reality that her parents were alive. A group of human rights' activists from both sides of the border had worked tirelessly to get her parents released.

As Nala waited for her parents at the border, she had many thoughts running through her mind. Her parents had not been able to be by Nala's side when she needed them. She was more familiar with the ways of her grandparents than her own parents. She did not get the benefit of their loving care during her entire childhood. She had to even give up her education for a while as a result of financial constraints. Life had played strange tricks on Nala.

There was a lot of emotion when mother and daughter united and later when father and daughter united. Her mother showed Nala, her newborn child. Nala's new sibling, in flesh and blood, was a cute darling. The little fellow was a darling with big bulging eyes.

Nala said, 'Mother, I am very happy to see you after such a long time. It has been ten years since I last saw you. I was ten when fate took away the two of you, from me. I have been a good girl.' Then looking sideways at her new sibling, she whispered softly into her mother's ears - 'These days, people say that I am singing very well, ma.' Nala was training rather well, in her efforts to become a classical singer.

Addressing her father, she said, 'I am so glad. You are back. Now all of us can start our lives anew. Yes?' Looking at her little brother, she asked, 'How old is he?'

Nala's father replied, 'One year old. We never imagined that we would be free again.'

Nala's mother said, 'I was afraid that things would have changed a lot. I am happy to be proved wrong. You are alive and well. What about my mother?'

Nala replied, 'Grandmother is well. All is well.'

Nala's mother continued, 'Yes, I thank God that all is well.' After all, what else could she say? Could she say to her daughter that her father and mother had been lodged in different prisons and that the guard on duty, outside her cell had exploited her and that it was his child (born to her during her incarceration), whom she had introduced to everyone as Nala's new sibling. There was nothing that they could do to punish him because a complaint of such a nature would only increase the bitterness between both the nations, which were already filled with hatred for each other! As a mother, she would be losing the respect of her daughter. She could never risk that. Nala's mother kept quiet.

Nala's mother asked, 'So, dear, tell me, how did you learn to sing? We don't even have a radio.'

Nala's grandmother, who was slightly deaf but who could hear at all appropriate times said, 'Oh dear! She used to learn by listening to the songs played on the street mike and the classical segment on radio. At first, I used to dissuade her from wasting her time but when I understood the utility of the so-called wasted time, I encouraged her to listen to the songs and write down the lyrics. Now, she is singing well and is a regular singer at all festivals. She is earning more and more from her music.'

Nala's parents were very proud of her. Her parents basked in the new found celebrity status of their daughter.

~ ~ ~

Meanwhile, Prithvi had not forgiven Narayana, although the latter had done no wrong to the former. As is the way with fate, Prithvi found his way to the same firm in which Narayana worked. Both of them had joined the same law firm as junior advocates. This law firm was a little bit different from the others. The partner of the law firm was a certain Mr. Khanna. His thoughts and ideas were bizarre but they fit in a world full of bizarre people. *The world is fond of such people, who make life interesting.* Mr. Khanna believed in enhancing the mental performance and overall sense of well being of his employees. He wanted every advocate in his firm to be happy. He wanted to keep them happy for he knew that their mental wellbeing would lead to the firm's material well being! He would often take his employees, out on picnics to beautiful places in the picturesque countryside. Once, he decided to take his team for a day out for a boating experience at a famous lake.

As luck often comes in the way of sinners {though it is paradoxical!}, Mr. Khanna asked his employees to go in pairs. When they reached the Bambino Lake, Prithvi told Narayana, 'I want to go with you.' Of course, he had already re-awakened his friendship with the latter during the bus journey to the lake. When their boat was somewhere near the centre of the lake, Prithvi suddenly pushed Narayana into the lake. There was nobody around. 'As good as dead,' he thought. He could easily tell others that Narayana had found something in the waters and had leaned over to look at it.

When he came back to the shores, an extremely visibly upset Narayana was there waiting for Prithvi. Although Prithvi was shell-shocked to see Narayana, he did not show it. His anxiety-ridden mind thought,

'If this man says it all, I will lose my name, my family and all.'

~ ~ ~

Narayana welcomed Prithvi with a firm hand-shake as he got down from the dirt-ridden American alligator-sized boat.

Prithvi took sick leave for a few days after which, he returned back to work at the law firm. Surprisingly, Narayana didn't expose the misdeed of Prithvi. This unexpected treatment of the evil action with a virtuous reaction had the effect of turning Prithvi from an enemy to a friend. His behaviour changed drastically. *The transition from evil to good was visible. It is easy to be vicious for to be virtuous, one must develop resilience to temptation.*

Later when, Prithvi begged Narayana to forgive him and accept his friendship, the latter obliged. Narayana however remained wary of this new friendship and was not moved by the proclamation of deep and faithful friendship by Prithvi. Narayana thought that perhaps, Prithvi had not really changed. After all, how often do you find an evil person turn into a good soul? When Narayana's marriage to Nala was announced, Prithvi's joy was boundless. Prithvi treated Nala like his own sister and he worked very hard in organizing the marriage celebration. Nala marvelled at the profound friendship between her husband and the enigmatic Prithvi. Narayana never discussed about the reality of his relationship with Prithvi in the presence of his wife.

One day, Narayana received the news that Prithvi had drowned while saving a little child, who had accidentally fallen into the Bembana Lake. Narayana thought, 'Why did he go there? Why was the lake, a silent spectator?' The truth is that nature possesses a complete sense of judgment and justice, superior to even human beings. Narayana was often heard saying to his family, 'This is fate. When one does wrong, one might be saved and one does right, one might be punished. What we receive is often not what we deserve and what we deserve is often not what we receive. Yet, that does not change the truth, for the truth is eternal and beautiful.' The rich father of the poor drowned soul did not even turn up to perform the last rites as per Hindu traditions. The onus finally fell on Narayana to perform Prithvi's last rites. Narayana did not feel any remorse for Prithvi's fate and yet, he performed the Hindu last rites, flawlessly. All who had assembled for the last passage spoke appreciatively of Narayana and called him Prithvi's best friend. But Narayana did not question them. As the funeral pyre began to burn, it started to drizzle lightly. The lightness of the weather was a sharp contrast to Narayana's heart, which was heavy with memories. Back home, Narayana was consoled by his wife.

Soon after Prithvi's demise, Nala fell sick and had to be admitted to a nearby hospital situated on the 7$^{\text{th}}$ Main road of the 'Green' city. She could not forget Prithvi, who had been very affectionate towards her. She felt as if she had lost a brother.

~ ~ ~

'Ma…. Pa…. ba…. ba.' The baby was cooing. Nala's baby brother was announcing the completion of its first two successful years of joy in the human plane of existence; earth. Nala was very proud of her baby brother.

During one of the many evenings, when the sky showed off the beauty of its vibrant colours to the world, something happened. A Sunday evening saw Nala in deep conversation with her mother.

'So, tell me mother, what was the kind of the treatment that you received in prison? Were they very cruel or did they show a little bit of sympathy?' asked Nala. Nala noticed a cloud pass over her radiant mother's face and she sensed a sense of fear in her mother. Nala wanted to know the reason for this sudden bout of fear in her mother. She questioned her mother about what was bothering her. Nala asked, 'Mother, what happened? Speak to me.'

Nala didn't like her mother's silence. The next few sentences that her mother spoke plunged Nala into the deep sea of gloom and her happy existence seemed to have been suddenly interrupted by the surge in some of the older and familiar emotions of fear and despair - emerging as renewed threats!

A few minutes earlier, her mother had spoken. Her mother had said, 'The time has come for me to reveal certain facts to you. You are aware of the fact that your father and I were lodged in a prison in our neighbouring country. The prison officials were not considerate. They were not cruel but they were not sympathetic either. We were given food twice a day and it was bad food. It was quite intolerable. I can say that for sure. Life in jail is unpredictable. It can be so bad that you could actually be having the guard of your jail ask you for sexual favours. On one of those totally unpredictable days, the guard outside my cell raped me!'

Looking directly at Nala, her mother raised her voice and said. 'This brother is your half-brother. Forgive me!'

She continued saying, 'The guard has given me an unbearable life-time burden. Your father and I were lodged in the same prison but in different cells. Your brother is not your full-brother. He is only your half-brother!'

Nala was stunned at the revelation and felt a sudden desire to avoid the conversation, all together.

'Did they give you blankets on cold winter nights?' asked Nala.

'No, but then they gave us a thick and warm mat to sleep on and that was enough,' replied her mother.

'Did you often think of me, mother? Did you miss me?' asked Nala.

Nala's mother didn't reply. Her thoughts were pre-occupied. Nala's mother spoke in a low tone. 'Life will prepare you for many harsh truths. You must never reveal to the world what I have told you. Your tongue must be completely under your control. You must forgive me for hiding the truth from you. The circumstances were such and I had no choice. Please do forgive me. I may be your mother but I need your support and respect. I was only a victim of circumstances. I did no wrong, wantonly.'

Nala replied, 'Why should I forgive you? You have done no wrong. It is only the guard who must seek forgiveness from you. You might think that I wish that he be hanged. I don't want him to be hanged. Let us forgive him. Forgiveness clears our soul of unnecessary agony.'

Nala's mother was proud that her daughter had matured so very well over the years. The baby felt proud, too. The fire of hatred was extinguished for good.

# CHAPTER

# *Seven*

# *A Wish Fulfilled*

One day, Preetha was busy writing stories in her house. Suddenly, there was a loud knock on the door. Preetha had no intention of opening the door. She didn't like being disturbed at this late hour. Nevertheless, she covered the short distance to the front door in four fast brisk steps. She opened the door. An old man stood outside. 'May I come in?' asked the stranger in a feeble voice.

The writer said, 'I won't let in, strangers.'

The old man said, 'I am a stranger, of course but I am no rogue. Believe me, madam. I won't trouble you. I come here, on behalf of a charitable organization. You need not fear me. Now, may I come in?'

Preetha, for the sake of politeness had to invite him in. The old man took the cosiest seat in the hall. He began to speak in a low and monotonous tone. 'Madam, my name is Jaykrishnan. I work for a charitable trust, 'New Foundation'. It is an NGO. It is located on 4$^{th}$

Main road, Bandra market. We perform surgeries, free of cost for the underprivileged. Can you contribute to its fund, Madam? Please! We also do other charitable work like helping people affected by natural calamities. I heard that you are a writer. You must be pretty famous and rich!'

Preetha replied, 'I cannot give you much money because I don't have much now. I will definitely help your foundation when I earn more. I am just starting to become a little known. What I earn from taking tuitions is not able to cover even my basic utility bills. I don't have any God-father. Only God can help me now. I am not aware of the direction in which my life is heading. Now, leave immediately for God's sake.' Preetha's voice was growing louder and louder. The old man spoke haltingly, 'Madam, why should you be despondent?' The old man wore a weird smile on his visage as he spoke the words. At the sight of the weird smile of the old man, some old and overwhelming memories came gushing back in Preetha's mind. Preetha started to speak again. 'Had you been in my place, you would have felt the same way. Destiny is very powerful, much more powerful than what we think and more powerful than man,' Preetha continued. 'Man has many desires but one needs the support of luck to win. I have been writing for so long but I have not got anybody as yet to publish my book. Nobody wants to experiment with new talent. Man proposes and God disposes.'

The old man said, 'I am sure that somebody will bear the costs of publishing your book. You write very well. You are a talented writer and talent always attracts admiration. I am sure that any of your admirers will be willing to financially assist you, so that you may bring your works to the attention of the public.'

Preetha retorted angrily, 'Will you?'

The old man said, 'My dear sister, if you had not waited for such a long time to ask me, this matter would have been settled long ago. Man proposes and God does not always oppose.'

Preetha recognized the familiar voice. 'Victor! Are you playing a trick on me?' asked Preetha.

Victor smiled and replied, 'Faithfully yours, ma'am.'

Preetha was overjoyed. The following days and months were full of hectic activities ranging from proof reading, typing and printing. It was a big day for Preetha when she received the first copy of her book. It had a beautiful book cover. Victor was proving to be a good marketing manager for Preetha. To Preetha, it seemed to be rather unbelievable that Victor could possess good marketing skills in addition to being an excellent actor. Her book was soon on its way to becoming a bestseller with a little help from Victor's marketing skills. Success was finally Preetha's, as she had always envisaged. Preetha thought, 'Success is like a moody woman, who might unveil her face slowly but when she sees those with initiative and enterprise, she shows her face wholly and unselfishly.'

~ ~ ~

Now, Kasturi had two cousin sisters: Mala and Martha. Mala was a very beautiful and intelligent girl. Martha had her own unique qualities. The fact was that Mala was a girl who could find happiness in just about everything. She had a large number of friends who were very jovial and voluble, who were capable of discussing just about everything under the sun without going into the details of any issue. Mala spent many years in this pleasant fashion- in the midst of liars, idiots and misguiding friends. Then a day came when the final examination results were out and all others had been meted out a fair deal. All her friends had made it to the superior courses and superior colleges while she had not. Then, when her father fell sick, none of her friends volunteered to provide any support. Her father recovered after a year's gap. Mala's mind, however, never recovered its old state of joy. She decided to become a woman hermit in order to cut herself off from the world, which had been so unkind to her. No sooner had she started living the life of a woman hermit, she realized that just being a woman hermit would not free her from the troubles of life. She was surprised that many of the women hermits were not as free from mental burdens as she had thought they would be. She returned to the normal human fold. A few months of living among the people, rejuvenated her belief that the woman hermits were at least better than ordinary people. She reconverted into the sanyasa fold or monkhood. Martha tried to dissuade Mala but soon realized that all her attempts were in vain. Martha just didn't know how to convince her sister. Her own personality was not forceful and she knew that only a forceful personality has the power of bringing about a change in others. Perhaps, it would require a personality as forceful as Preetha to bring Mala into the normal fold, again.

# CHAPTER

## *Eight*

## *Shree Jay*

A little girl was running on the road near a public park in the Green City. A big dog was chasing her and it had an intense desire to bite the little child. **A hungry creature is an angry creature.** A cheerful young man, seventeen springs old, who was eating grapes, saw the sight and unlike many others, who ran away from the commotion - he quickly picked up several large pebbles and pelted them one by one at the animal. The dog left its original target and started to chase the young man. The young man, Shree Jay took one look at the fierce dog and ran like an Olympic champion. He climbed the first tree, which came his way. It was autumn season and the tree was shedding its leaves. Its dry leaves, each a bit of brown, yellow and green fell on the dog. Shree Jay kept pelting pebbles at the dog. The fourth pebble mortally wounded the poor animal. It tottered and fell and the leaves buried it. The young man, being a God-fearing person, prayed to God to forgive him for pelting pebbles at the poor animal to save the child. This was the first time that Shree Jay had to resort to violence. 'Of course, it was for a good cause,' he thought.

Shree Jay had a degree but no job. In fact, he was looking for one and he was lucky that Preetha was one of those who regularly went to the park for her morning walk. She thought the young man must be bold and approached him, in order to congratulate him for his act of courage in helping the young child. During that time, Preetha was in need of a personal assistant-cum-secretary. Shree Jay seemed to fit the bill. So, Preetha told him about her requirement and Shree immediately accepted the job offer.

Meanwhile, Kasturi being a hater of men since childhood, had married quite late. But her husband left her soon after marriage. Unknown to her, the mental strain had produced a physical impact on her. Her weak mind led to many physical weaknesses and she could not effectively perform even her household functions. She was later affected by other physical ailments, too. She could barely stand or sit and could not sleep at all. She had begun to hallucinate as a result of her disturbed psychology and physical illnesses. Soon, she developed the habit of unconsciously getting down from the bed, at nights and sleeping on the floor. When the problems persisted, she gathered courage and overcame her hesitation and called up her friend, Preetha. When Preetha heard over the phone, as to what had happened, she ordered Shree Jay to provide his services to her friend and sent him to Kasturi's home near the mountains.

Kasturi had many obsessive thoughts. She always kept wondering about the various components of universe: asteroids, meteors, meteorites, black holes, planets, stars, galaxies and universes. Kasturi was so weak with over-thinking that she could hardly walk up to open the front door of her house. Shree Jay was overjoyed to see Kasturi. She was the girl, who had lived on the street adjoining his own, during his adolescent days! He had loved Kasturi from childhood but had never ever expressed his love to Kasturi, knowing well, her antagonism to all men. When he did want to express his feelings, it was all too late. Another man had proposed to Kasturi and she had accepted the latter suitor. A delighted Shree Jay spoke. 'I am Preetha madam's assistant. She has sent me to take care of you.' Kasturi had not seen him for many years, now. It was not surprising that she could not recognise him. After all, his facial features had changed quite a bit. He had struggled and suffered in the intermittent years. His face had lost its sheen.

On the very first day, Shree Jay tried to help out Kasturi. 'Is the grinder in the kitchen?' he asked. 'Yes, it is there,' replied Kasturi. He went and ground some herbs and added the same in buttermilk and gave the concoction to her. She felt much better. He repeated it, every four hours for the next several days. Within a few days, she became better. He cooked her meals. He cooked the rice with a little more water and gave her curd rice to eat, twice a day with steamed vegetables. Every day, he gave her tender coconut water to drink and she began to recover very fast. Every evening, he used to switch on the tape recorder and put the tapes of both eastern and western music. Music can change the mood of the person and Kasturi used to feel pleased on hearing the lovely tunes. Her jaundice subsided as his caring attitude intensified. Kasturi was pleased. She said to Shree Jay, 'You seem to know a lot. Are you a naturopathy doctor?'

Shree Jay replied, 'No, Madam. I am not. I learnt all this from my grandmother. My grandmother always believed that if nature cannot cure, nothing else can. Nature is an undeniable truth. No one can go against nature and survive.' Shree Jay was elder to Kasturi by a decade and Kasturi began to look upon Shree as her own elder brother.

# CHAPTER

## *Nine*

## *Shree Jay's Past Comes Back*

Gola Gampha. It was an area where many rickshawwallahs and their families, lived. The days in Gola Gampha were never happy for one reason - the rickshawwallahs' days of work meant unending pain in the limbs, sweat, dirt and reality. They were some rickshaw-wallahs, who used to pull the rickshaws with their torsos and there were others, who used to pedal the cycle. The other reason was that the weather was never bright and shining. The days were always dull and cloudy. They were happier, when the day would get over and the closing twilight brought with it, cheap liquor and meandering music from the nearby marriage hall. The music blaring from the mikes of the marriage hall was their connection with the world of music and cinema. *Music is a strange person for it can make you smile or cry, thrill you or scare you like a human being.*

Every night, the music from the hall took them on a roller coaster ride of emotions. Every day, after ferrying the passengers back and forth to destinations, it was with an expected joy with which they used to listen to the songs. The music was always adulterated; intercepted as it was by car horns, auto horns, human speech and screams. Every morning, they used to get up to perform a daily ritual, which was to catch a duck from somewhere and throw it up in the air so that it would land on the road, to be crushed by a speeding posh car. After the car would hit the bird, they would stop the car and terrorise the chauffeur and other passengers of the car and harass them in order to compel them into parting with some solid cash and this money was always honestly shared amongst them and it served as a supplement to their paltry incomes. Very often, the additional sum went to pay the cost of tickets to watch the movies of their favourite stars at the nearby cinema theatre.

Shree Jay, meanwhile, was proving to be a very competent secretary to Preetha. She had given him money in order to pay to learn car driving which he did in a short time and thus, Shree Jay combined the duties of an honest driver and competent secretary.

One day, Preetha asked her chauffeur, Jay, to take her to the hotel 'L'Homme Heureurx'. She had to deliver an important lecture on 'The Importance of Quality in Contemporary Writing.' It was around six in the morning when they meandered through Gola Gampha. The local ruffians threw a duck and it landed in front of the car in which Preetha was travelling. The rickshawwallahs gathered around the car immediately and one tall fellow, Mr. King screamed, 'What have you done? You have killed him. He was such a friendly fellow. He was one of us.'

Preetha was a lover of birds and animals. She was extremely unhappy over the incident but she was definitely unprepared for this blatant and unnatural description - the personification a duck! Meanwhile, the rickshawwallahs were mentally preparing some strategies to extract a good deal of money from her. The rickshawwallahs, however, had not as yet seen the chauffeur, as the windows of the car were pitch dark; as it happens with all the cars of the high and the mighty. When the windows of the car were rolled up, they saw Shree Jay. Almost immediately, a tall rickshaw-wallah said, 'We are sorry, madam. This is our trick and we do it daily.' Another rickshaw wallah, a man with a dark scar on his face said, 'We throw ducks before big cars and extract money from the driver and other passengers. Please forgive us.'

Preetha forgave them and left. The next day morning, Shree Jay went to meet the rickshawwallahs at Gola Gampha. 'I suppose Madam was very impressed with your honesty for she has deposited one thousand rupees in each of your fifty names in the bank and from now on, you will get ten percent of it as your interest every year. A thousand rupees, a year! Are you hearing?'

The ears of the rogues were up like rabbits. It was the news of a lifetime. They praised Madam's generosity and many of them asked Shree Jay, 'Jay, is it true?' When Jay confirmed the good news that Madam Preetha had, in truth, deposited in their names, the given sum of money, they erupted in joy.

Shree Jay hurried to Preetha's mansion and went straight up to her and said, 'Madam, you gave me, a good-for-nothing fellow, trust and a job. I have cheated you. Forgive me!' Preetha was completely taken aback and she asked, 'Why should I forgive you?' What have you done?'

Shree Jay replied, 'Madam, before coming to work here, I was a part-time rickshaw wallah. My days as a rickshaw wallah brought me close to those, whom you met yesterday. I have spent over a year of my life in Gola-Gampha. I know that you must have been impressed by their honesty yesterday but actually they were trying to save their skin for they believed that I would spill the truth of my being their former comrade in injustice and crime and would list out their dishonourable deeds.'

Preetha asked, 'I suspected all this from the beginning. When the rickshawwallahs blurted the truth, I suspected that something was amiss. Why should they speak the truth? Their eyes conveyed a deep sense of fear when they looked at you. I sent a trusted man to verify the facts and he gathered information about you and he told me about everything, yesterday itself. By the way, why do you think, I gave them the money?'

Shree was surprised and Shree replied, 'It is your generous nature, madam.'

Preetha said, 'I did it for the ducks. I was having obsessive dreams. I couldn't sleep in the night thinking of those ducks, reaching the heavens, one after the other; every morning dashed by the four-wheeled predatory metal monsters. I did it for myself.' Shree Jay walked away, quite bewildered. 'So, it was not a feeling of generosity, which had prompted Preetha to perform the act but something else!,' thought Shree Jay to himself. *Truth is indeed, often stranger than fiction.*

# CHAPTER

## *Ten*

## *Saviour Friend*

Mr. Victor had had, meanwhile, three movie flops in a row and his movie career was in jeopardy. With unkind film critics and the sliding of his career, he was no longer able to get good offers and with the kind of stuff happening in his life, he was depressed. A lonely personal life led Victor to the habit of using methylamphetamine but the greatest relief of Victor's life was to come in the form of his sister, Preetha.

Preetha came to visit Victor, intermittently. During her visits to Victor's home, she often found him in a strange state of mind but Victor was neither seeking any medical nor psychological care out of fear of bad publicity. After all, a movie star's entire career is completely dependent on the image of the star in the minds of the public, which is created by the media and Victor did not want the media to create any phantom about him. His fragile mind began to wander into the trammelling tunnel of depression. *Depression is a terrible monster. It eats up a person slowly, without his knowledge.* One day, while preparing a lunch for Victor, she observed his shoes, which were in a corner. They were unusually dirty and unpolished. She thought, 'This is strange. Victor always polishes his shoes.'

She sat on his opposite side, across the table when Victor was eating and looked at him in the eye. When there is a need to extract the truth from a person, an investigator must look at the person's eye and ask the necessary question. Of all the parts of the human body, the eyes are the strangest. With their expressions, they are complete individuals in themselves. Only the eyes reveal the true sentiments of a person. When Preetha asked Victor to speak the truth, looking at him in the eye, Victor revealed the pain that he was hiding. Preetha said, 'If you take doses of methyl amphetamine, a banned narcotic to make you forget your failures, then what must people take to forget their sufferings? Do all people have the luck of attaining all that they want? The ones, who have the capacity to take failures, successfully in their stride, are the ones, who succeed in the huge activity that is life. Life is not worth losing. We must learn to fight and win. Victory is for those who persist in their endeavours. We will win. You will win. We will win, together. The greatest of challenges can be overcome by displaying unity in the face of adversity. What do you say? Do you agree with me?'

Victor explained, 'My dear sister! If everyone gets a guide like you in life, everyone will succeed in life.'

Preetha soon moved into Victor's house and started to take care of him. She cared for him with the tenderness of a mother. His health recovered quickly with the healthy food, loaded with vegetables and fruits that Preetha had prepared, combined with her divine touch. Little changes in his make-up, dress and hairstyle as well as selection of good roles saw Victor's career once again soaring to great heights. Meanwhile, the usual rounds of gossip began again and Preetha decided to call on her friend, Kasturi. The two together discussed on how to solve Victor's loneliness once and for all. 'Yes, marriage would be the panacea for all his problems,' concluded Kasturi.

With confused thoughts fluttering through her mind, Preetha asked Kasturi, 'But, where will I find a bride for my brother? There are not many young women whom I know.' Then turning towards Kasturi, Preetha asked, 'Will you help me? Is there anyone known to you, who wouldn't mind marrying a cine star? It must be someone who would be able to put up with the queerness of cine stars and their lives. It must be someone who would not mind seeing her husband with other women in the course of acting. I mean someone who can make a clear distinction between real life and cinema.'

Kasturi deliberated deeply and spoke. 'I have two cousin sisters, Mala and Martha. Mala is a woman hermit, who has taken the vow of celibacy and therefore cannot marry. Martha is well educated and intelligent.

She is a person with a broad outlook and will definitely not mind marrying a cine star. I will ask her. She will marry Victor and lend stability to his life.'

Kasturi went to Martha's home to ask her whether she could marry Victor.

Martha replied, 'Of course, I will not. He must be really a bad fellow if he is into movies. He must be morally weak man. Even if he had ever been a virtuous man, it is not possible for him to remain like that in his chosen work place, which is cinema. He would have surely acted in many intimate scenes with several heroines and it is quite unlikely that the trend will not continue in his future ventures.'

'I don't know about others but he must be a good person if Preetha says so. She is very honest,' said Kasturi.

When Martha didn't give her consent, Kasturi went back to Preetha and explained the turn of events.

'Tell me about Mala. Why did she become a woman hermit?' enquired Preetha. Kasturi replied, explaining the unhappy turn of events in Mala's life, which made her feel bitter with the rest of humanity. Preetha listened carefully and said, 'I want to meet her. Where can I find her?'

Kasturi said, 'Are you out of your mind? She is a woman hermit and that too, one who came back to the normal human fold and then had gone to the sanyasa life, for good. There is no chance of being able to convince her.'

Preetha said, 'I will convince her.' Kasturi said simply, 'She is in Ritumela. You will find her in the Rakshaka mutt there.'

Preetha thanked Kasturi for the information and packed up her bags. She put on a false wig so that nobody could identify her and hurriedly, fixed a big black false mole on her cheeks before catching the first bus from Madruga bus stand to Ritumela.

It was a crowded bus but one sharp fellow seemed to recognize her and yes, he was a journalist. He closely nudged his way to stand beside her and asked her in soft whispers, 'Madam, what are you doing? A grand escapade! Please tell me, what's going on. Allow me to interview you.'

Preetha replied, 'Allow me to go in peace. Give me your telephone number, Sir. When I get back home, I will contact you and give you a complete interview. This is no scandal. I have personal work to do and I cannot tolerate any interference at this juncture. I hope that you will believe me when I say that I do not wish to be disturbed.

When it appeared that the journalist did not believe her, she gave him her visiting card and wrote the following words behind the visiting card, 'I promise the bearer, an interview'. She signed on the card and handed it over to the journalist.

It was in the evening that she reached Ritumela. Ritumela was a bustling pilgrim centre where hundreds of thousands of devotees took dips in the holy waters of the river, Amba, everyday. It was the belief of the devotees that a dip in the river would lead them to salvation, impromptu. Not the one to miss an opportunity, Preetha took a dip in the river as soon as she arrived, praying to the great Gods to grant her success in her earnest endeavour to unite two good human beings in wedlock. She prayed to God to grant her friend-brother, success and peace. She prayed for everyone. Preetha believed that the whole world was one family. After completing her prayers, she stepped out of the river, went back to her room in the hotel, wore a saffron coloured sari (another of her ideas, to please Mala) and took an auto rickshaw to the Rakshaka Mutt.

After making inquiries about Mala at the Rakshaka Mutt, Preetha found her way to Mala. Mala was beautiful and kind looking. Almost instantaneously, Preetha decided that Mala would make the ideal better half for Victor. Preetha was determined not to lose in this endeavour of match-making. She smiled at her own determination.

Preetha said, 'Hello, Mala. My name is Preetha and I am your cousin, Kasturi's best friend. Perhaps, you might have heard about me.' In a voice of quiet and gentle firmness, Preetha continued, 'I am also a writer of some prominence, you could say.'

Mala retorted, 'What cousin? I have no cousin. I have severed all my relationships with the world. I am a woman hermit, don't you know?'

Preetha said, 'Of course, I do know that. I don't deny it. Kasturi informed me, about your upbringing and how you resorted to this conversion to sanyasa in order to escape from the problems of this world.'

'What do you want?' asked Mala.

Preetha asked, 'Why did you become a woman hermit? Was it your desire to serve humanity, which made you to become a woman hermit?'

'No,' replied Mala.

Preetha questioned her further. 'Did you have any vision of God which prompted you to leave the material world?' enquired Preetha of Mala.

Mala again replied in the negative.

Preetha asked, 'So, why did you do this?'

Mala said, 'I did it because I was unhappy. That's it.'

Shri was unrelenting and determined. But Preetha was equally determined to have her way. She replied, 'I thought you had turned to monkhood as a means of attaining spirituality. Becoming a monk is not just a means of searching for spirituality for oneself but it also becomes a means of spreading spirituality for others. No one should become a monk for selfish reasons. No. I don't think that is right. So, I don't think that you have done well either for yourself or to others by becoming a monk. Monkhood is not for you. If unhappiness is what it takes for a person to take to Sanyasa, then the whole world would have been full of hermits. Now, tell me if there is anyone in this cosmos, who is perfectly happy? You will have to listen to me. You are just twenty-two! Don't ruin yourself. Life is beautiful. Come and live your life. You deserve to live joyously.

There is no escape from the realities of life. One has to stand up to face the challenges of life. Only a truly realised soul finds peace in sanyasa; one who wants to serve mankind. Otherwise, only cowards take to this recourse in order to create a false ambience of peace and solitude for their disturbed souls.'

Mala replied, 'Who are you to render me advice? I did not ask you for any advice. You are going, beyond your limits. Stop it! Please, leave me alone.'

Preetha replied, 'I will stop but not until you hear everything that I have got to say. You are young. You have an entire life before you. You have no right to waste it when someone could do a lot better with your support. What is the point in being selfish? It takes valour to live for others. Only cowards live for themselves. Your celibacy is of no purpose. It is going to benefit no one. Even you are not enjoying the benefits of physical celibacy because I get the feeling that you are not able to resist the mental images of enjoyment. There is someone who has suffered like you and who needs you.' Preetha told Mala about Victor.

Preetha said, 'Think about it. I will return to Ritumela after a month. I hope you will be able to change your mind, by then. Don't waste your life in futility. Life is precious, more precious than you think.' This sudden bombardment of sensible advice infused in Mala, a new wave of excitement, which left her in a confused state of mind. 'What should I do', she wondered. After Preetha left the place, Mala was in a state of mild shock.

After her mind had settled down a bit, Mala spoke to Kasturi. She discussed with her cousin, in detail about all that Preetha had said.

Meanwhile, Preetha went back to her hometown. The journalist called her up, almost immediately. 'Madam, what about the interview that you had promised to grant me?'

Preetha said, 'I will do as I promised. I need a month's time. There is an important issue, which I have to attend to, first. It involves my perseverance and confidence.'

*The journalist promised to give her a month's time.*

Ten days later, she received a call from Mala, who said, 'I am thinking. I need time.'

Preetha waited patiently. Five days later, on a friday morning, Preetha received the wonderful message from Mala, which she had awaited and which had cost her, several sleepless nights. Preetha was ecstatic. What a success! She had convinced Mala to marry Victor.

She rewarded the journalist with an interview of his lifetime. Several appreciated Preetha's contribution to Victor's life, a person who was not related to her by blood but by love. Preetha said quite simply, in her interview, 'There are many philosophers, scientists, discoverers, inventors, freedom fighters and philanthropists who have all contributed to our lives, knowingly and unknowingly and whose goodness we can never repay. In comparison, my own contribution to a person's life to one who has been like a brother to me is quite small. I did only my duty. It has given me happiness.'

# CHAPTER
## *Eleven*

## *The Most Powerful Man*

Jnankeshwara was a learned scholar. He was an urbanite and a very confident person with clear priorities- when it came to his own issues. He had his own principles and preference of emotions. However he was always confused when confronted with societal issues. He had no qualms about disturbing people to ascertain **the truths of life**. Though by nature he was a very merry man, of late, he had been struck by many doubts and had become a serious thinker. At this moment, he was trying to find out as to who the most powerful person in the country was. This, he was trying to do by private investigation, using the scientific method of sampling. Of course, all this research was unnecessary. But then how do you distinguish between useful and unnecessary research. 'But then research must be conducted whether there are benefits to society or not. Is it not so?' he thought and decided to go all over the country, through villages, cities, towns, mountains, forests and deserts asking people belonging to different occupations as to who, according to them was or were the most important man or men respectively. It could even be termed as the battle of the occupations.

Keshwara set out. He did not want to make use of any modern conveyance. Though he was an urbanite, his notions were traditional and conservative. He decided to go on foot to the distant nooks and corners of his nation in order to find out as to who the most powerful man was or men were. He wanted to know the truth, the hard way. Till this point of time, nobody had done much to ease the difficulties of the travelers. However, the tall trees shading the long roads on both sides benefited Jnan by providing him a steady supply of fruits and shade.

Ganga Nagar was his first halt. It was a small village in the district of D'Salem. It was a sparsely populated region, for the people were only beginning to awaken to a new world, after the devastating earthquake, which had struck it many years ago. After entering the village, Jnankeshwara was struck by the quietness of the place. He noticed a young villager squatting on the ground, looking at a disappearing lake. Years of pollution in the form of industrial wastes and chemicals had deadened the lake. It was unfit for drinking. The water used by the people of the village was carcinogenic but death caused by cancer was preferable to dying of thirst. The young man was in no mood to answer questions but Jnankeshwara was determined to decipher the truth. Success comes to those who show perseverance.

'Tell me, who is the most important person according to you?' asked Jnankeshwara.

'Undoubtedly, it is the village Collector. He represents the Government. He works for our welfare,' said Mammu. Then Mammu's friend gesticulated to him to come over to his side. Mammu said, 'I have to go. You must excuse me. We have other work to do than just answering you people who come to the rural areas and do stupid surveys.' Noticing the sad look on the investigator's face, Mammu quickly changed his demeanour and rendered his sincere apologies and then went away.

The investigator hurried back to Venkaih's hut. Jnan was staying with him. Venkaih was a farmer and was more prosperous than others in his village. He was one of those educated farmers, who used modern technology in farming combining it with certain other traditional farming methods. It was no surprise that the other farmers didn't like him. They were all very jealous of him. That night, Jnankeshwara was served with hot chapattis, steaming white rice, fried and salted bitter gourd and curds. The hot weather had just given way to evening cool winds with light rains and a lovely earthy fragrance began to waft in the air. Thus, eating such hot and spicy food on the cold floor was quite a pleasure both to the hosts and the guests.

Venkaih's wife began to speak, 'I hope you like our village?'

Jnankeshwara replied, 'Yes, but the people here are very poor.'

Venkaih said, 'Yes. I wish a saviour could come to save us.'

Jnankeshwara replied 'Indeed! I do think your people need saviours.'

Venkaih said, 'Jnanji, why do you wear these clothes? They are not good for your health. They can cause skin problems and prevent sweating. Wear cotton clothes like us. It is much more healthy, cooling and comfortable to wear in this tropical climate.'

Jnankeshwara replied 'Ah! I understand.'

That night, Jnankeshwara borrowed some clothing from the host and wore it and went to sleep. For the first time, in years, he slept well.

The next day, after thanking the Venkaih family, Jnankeshwara walked towards his next stop, Balganga Nagar. As he was walking towards this prosperous village, whose dynamic district commissioner had transformed it into a place filled with livestock and schools, Jnankeshwara swooned. The mad hot weather had affected his head. A kind villager passing by in his cycle, got down from his bicycle, climbed up a coconut tree, plucked a tender coconut, had it cut open and poured the fresh and juicy contents into the throats of the urbanite. A recovered Jnankeshwara did not want to lose this opportunity, too. After thanking his benefactor, he repeated his question. 'Sir, I am doing research. Can you tell me as to who is the most important person in the world?'

The other man hastily replied, 'My landlord.'

Jnan encountered with a 'Why?'

The villager said, 'He has provided me with employment and employment means money, which means I can buy products. Employment opportunities cannot be easily created. Do you think that people should fight more in order to have more gun sellers, more police stations, more police, more courts and more judges? Do you think more people should fall sick, so that more doctors can be properly employed? Do you think we should produce commodities of low quality so that there will be more replacement demand leading to greater production? This employment generation problem is not always as easy to solve as we think.'

Jnan said, 'That's a view-point. All right. I must go now. Bye.'

Although earlier, Jnan had planned to go to Balganga Nagar, he now felt that there was no need to do so. He proceeded towards Antaryani Nagar. Antaryani Nagar had a temple and the life of Antaryani Nagar evolved around the temple. Currently, thousands of workers were busy renovating the temple. A village fair was to begin soon and different varieties of sweets were to be put up in the stalls along with spicy food. Production was in full swing. The whole town reverberated with the sounds of trumpets, tables, shehnais, sitars, sarods, sarangis, flute, carnatic and Hindustani music.

Jnan asked for directions to the headman's house. The Headman of the village was Dharani. Dharani was asked the same question 'You city people have got nothing better to do. Why do you disturb our tranquillity? Please go away.'

The investigator persisted, 'Sir, please...'

'To me, the people of my village and their progeny are the most important people in the world and that includes my progeny too,' said Dharani and smiled. A few kilometres from where Jnan was standing, began the cold Manjaro Mountains. Jnan thought it to be a fairly good idea to go and interview some mountain folk in the context of his research. He wanted to make his study more broad-based. Soon afterwards, Jnankeshwara began to make adequate preparations before the departure to the mountains. He had planned to stay there for two days. The first day was spent in establishing friendly contacts with the lonely mountain men for Jnan considered it rather prudent to establish a friendly relationship with the mountain folk before venturing out in order to question them regarding their priorities.

By the first evening, he was able to befriend a man called Sim. It is interesting to note the manner in which Sim and Jnan met. Jnan saw a man climbing down, one of the many Manjaro hills. He was an enormously fat man and Jnan could not restrain himself and burst out laughing. Minutes later, he controlled his laughter and looking at the other man with a smug smile said, 'You look very prosperous. You must forgive me for my plain speaking. I am a bit of a simpleton. I did not mean to be insolent.' The man, Sim took an instant liking to the researcher and allowed him to stay with him in his mountain cottage. After a few introductory remarks and talks, Jnan hurriedly asked his question. Sim said, 'To me, my neighbour, Tim is the most important person in the country because he gives me charcoal to keep my belly, warm and as well as to keep my home, warm.' He then removed a wooden basket from beneath his clothing covering the area around his rotund belly. He then removed a pot of charcoal from within the basket and showed the burning charcoal to Jnankeshwara. 'We use this to keep ourselves warm,' said Sim.

After Sim left the place, Jnan went to meet Tim and repeated his question. 'As far as I am concerned, my neighbour, Sim is the most important person. We are lonely up in the mountains. Company is rare. There are very few people who live up here in the mountains. Where would I be without him? I can talk to him whenever I want. He is never moody and is always jocund. I could not have asked for a better neighbour. I have only one grievance against God. He could have made Sim richer. Poor Sim, I really sympathise with him.'

The next day, Jnan took leave of Sim and Tim and began his descent to the plains. Every now and then he turned back to see them, who were waving at him as Jnan descended down the hills till the latter disappeared into the plains He would probably never meet them again. Jnan could clearly hear the pounding of heart beat as he remembered the kindness that had been shown to him, by his new friends. Jnan proceeded to the plains towards Sajapura. He met Aaron, the famous poet of the region. Aaron was confronted by Jnan and was surprised to hear the question put forth by Jnankeshwara. 'Who, according to you is the most powerful person?' Aaron thought Jnan to be a strange man who had such a strange question to ask. However, he did not reveal his thoughts and proceeded to answer the question posed by our investigator.

'The most important person, in my opinion, is the artist. The world consisted only of objects and colours and was without language for a very long duration of time. Pictures are immortal and project the world in its correct native splendour.'

*Thus, people seemed to have a different opinion concerning the most important person in their life. Our dear investigator, however, was not the one to give up his goal easily and proceeded with confidence to wasting his energy in a very useless endeavour.*

In Diffinoor, the investigation interviewed another poet, who was also a very renowned writer. 'There can be no two opinions on the subject. The writers of a society are the most important people in a society. It is they who give meaning to objects and ideas. History, culture, civilization and all activities are finally representations of the written words and spoken sounds. Writers attain immortality through their writings. No other profession in the world can stake such a claim to pre-eminence.'

In Gunapur, a few kilometres away from Diffinoor, a sculptor was asked the same question, by our wise investigator. He said, 'I can sculpt something only out of matter but a writer alone can create a world with ideas. My work is tangible. A book is tangible. However, a work of art can be easily destroyed but even if a hard copy of a book gets destroyed, the words come to life again in some other form; often in the spoken form. As far as I am concerned - It stands as a brilliant testimony in history. The written words and the equivalent spoken forms are permanent. They live forever. Even though, I am a sculptor, I accept the superiority of the writing profession.'

A number of people felt that the politicians were the most important people since they were the decision makers. In the same society, when the politicians were asked, they swore that they owed allegiance only to the people. In their opinion, people were supreme. From here, Jnan decided to go to the cities. 'Would the urbanities think differently from the villagers?' wondered the thinker and he was not disappointed for each one of the urbanites, who were interviewed, had a different opinion regarding the complicated topic.

At Madhurapura, Jnan's first interviewee was a businessman. He said, 'The art of making money dates back to times immemorial. In spite of its great prowess, money is destructible. I should know. I am a businessman. Music is indestructible and hence, I feel that the group of musicians, composers, lyricists and singers are the most important. The world can live without businessmen but not without music. We could even revert back to the old system of barter but one cannot imagine a world sans the youthful spring of variegated music. Music is colours of waves and frequencies.' At Purushapuram, he met a singer who said, 'Life is a race for money. What is talent without wealth? The wealthiest man is the most important person to me.'

At Vagpura, an old man said, 'The most important man is the one who prints the currency notes at the Central Bank.' The illiterate man thought that the printer of the national currency notes had the right to print as many notes and of varying denomination as he desired! By now, Jnan was a truly bewildered man. He was thoroughly confused. He felt that it had been an act of madness to waste a whole year, doing something, which would benefit no one, not even himself. ***He realised that most research is futile.***

With these anguishing feelings choking him, Jnan strayed into a public meeting near Vagpura. The speaker was Preetha. She spoke outstandingly well and mesmerized the audience. Our investigator was mesmerized, too. At last, he had identified his most important person. He darted forward to meet the brilliant speaker. After a great deal of persuasion with the authorities, Jnan found himself directly speaking to Preetha about his experiences. Preetha laughed and asked, 'Who is the most important person according to you?'

Jnan replied, 'It is you.' A surprised Preetha began to explain - 'Philosophically, it is for an individual to recognise that one's own self is the most important person in one's life. In fact, what does the world mean to a person without the individual himself, in question? Every human being thus, formulates his conclusions based on his own individual set of assumptions derived from his unique set of experiences on every issue. As far as your research is concerned, I must say it has been an exercise in futility. Why did you spend your time in such a foolish endeavour? You could have spent the same amount of time in another endeavour, which could have been of benefit to society. Good research work is that body of work, which by providing newer insights on different issues, benefit society, leading to the greatest welfare and prosperity of all men. Today, most research work is misdirected and is a waste of time. As far as your question is concerned, in my opinion, it is the farmer, who is the most important person in society, for where would we be without food? In truth, there are many answers, which vary with time with changing situations. Truth alone is immortal. Virtue is immortal. All experiences may begin within the human body but they don't end there.'

'I have been a misguided youth all my life. I did not enjoy the tutelage of wise people. Now, I have learnt from you about maintaining clarity in thoughts, words and deeds. Will you take me as your disciple?' asked Jnan. Soon, Jnan began to accompany Preetha on all her tours. He faithfully followed his guru, everywhere.

# Twelve

## Sweet Jup

Jup was from Indonesia near the Saran Mountains in Borneo. In the beginning, life was beautiful. Its parents were very loving and cared a lot for their child. Home was mahogany, ebony, greenheart, cabinet woods and dyewoods. From the very top of its Mahogany tree home, it could watch a beautiful river, flowing in the deep valley, below! Jup led a very peaceful life. Everything was available at its doorstep. It led a very luxurious life in his densely decorated home, the forest. Unlike humans, it was never plagued by anger, unhappiness, jealousy, fear or disgust.

It knew only peace, happiness, beauty and compassion. Around a hundred and eighty species of trees were around it and the growing season was all the year round. Every tree had a pattern. At each instance of time, some plants flowered, some others bore fruit and some others decayed. The tropical rain forests of hardwood knew neither seasonality nor time. They had no visitors and no troubleshooters. Existence was lonely but fulfilling in this far away hidden corner of the earth. The trees were towering personalities and even twenty men could not equal to one of them. They set forth no terms and conditions, had no goals, made no losses, no gains and knew no pain. Time's compulsion on change was abrupt and slow. It woke up to bright mornings with happiness. It always ate well and would pick up fruits of different varieties and would savour them under his favourite bushes and trees. It would then return to a cozy corner of the branch of some pretty tree and wait for the rain God to shower his blessings on mankind. The rain God often endeared himself to those living near Saran by giving his blessings in plenty. The afternoons would pass in quiet action. Jup, the Orangutan made no investments on anything, had no expectations and expected life to remain with such intentions too.

There was a gunshot. A bullet lodged itself in Jup's right arm and it fell on the earth and into a new world. The bullet was removed and Jup found itself waiting in the pet market, for a master. A little boy bought Jup. The parents of the little boy pampered him a lot. Jup was the outcome of the resolution of the boy to buy it. The little boy played with it when he liked and the orangutan was left to itself at other times. Jup didn't hate the little boy but did not love him either. He just was there. Around that time, the family of the Mannans, the Indonesian family with whom Jup was staying, decided to migrate to another country. Their little boy wanted to take Jup with them but his parents did not prefer it that way. They warned their son of serious consequences but their threats had no effect on him, whose mind was fixated on his goal. He decided to have Jup smuggled. While the parents spent the next few months in buying products, meeting relations, settling accounts and arranging for finance, their little boy began to entertain hopes of being successfully able to smuggle the little animal aboard the ship. The arrangements of both parents and son were successful. Jup was not to be disappointed.

The orangutan was uncomfortable as it had to live the next several days in a small cage. Food was irregular and there were many other allied problems. Jup's little master had already secretly met the captain of the ship and had sought his permission. Though the captain knew the regulations, he decided to disobey them as he was impressed by the little boy's bravery and resoluteness. However, it was not only the little boy's bravery which had made him bring Jup along with him. It was in fact his sense of fear for he wanted to have company. He was afraid that the boys in the new land would not like him and he would be left friendless.

Jup reached his new destination in sickness and once they had landed there, his little master convinced his parents as to how terrible he felt for having left Jup behind. As soon as his parents began to succumb to the guilt, the little boy displayed his prized trophy, dear little Jup. The parents loaded Jup and their son into a vehicle and reached their new home. After a few days,

Jup's little master, started going to school and he made new friends at his new school and he forgot all about Jup. When the parents of the little boy noticed him losing interest in Jup, his parents, too began to evince little interest in the monkey.

Foxton, their new home was a quiet city on the east, near the hills. The weather became less warm and Jup became more intelligent. It understood that it was missing out on the larger experience of life. The beautiful hills were full of fragrant herbs and tall trees, which would suffuse the air with an exhilarating mix of sweet fragrances. But one day, the hilly weather became rather unbearable for our ape. It was then that Jup decided that the fragrant hills and a good master were insufficient for its progress. It was at that moment that Jup decided to leave his little master to go in search of newer experiences.

One fine day, it crossed the road like he saw the other people do. It waited for a bus like the other people did and soon got into a bus. It was soon touring the city. It was all very new to him. It changed buses often and on noticing that Jup was quiet and well behaved, there was always some kind fellow on every bus, who would pay for the ticket for the orangutan. A ticket to somewhere and to nowhere... Thus, little Jup became a common sight on buses, plying from place to place. Soon, Jup was far away from Foxton. Jup led a vagabond's life for some time. Some people, of course, tried to catch it but it was always able to dodge them. Some others threw pebbles at it. He dodged them, too. A few people were kind to it and obliged it with sweet eatables. Jup survived on their mercy.

At one point of time, Jup felt extremely tired because of hunger but then again, it felt invigorated when it saw the fruits of banana hanging from the trees. He helped himself to a few of them. It was at that moment that Kasturi noticed the orangutan. She was standing her home's kitchen, cooking her lunch, when she happened to spot the lone monkey. After reassuring herself of the good intentions of the monkey, she decided not to disturb it. Meanwhile, Jup had noticed this human being's gentleness and reciprocated by displaying good behaviour; an uncharacteristic feature of simian; after all, it had been a human child's pet for quite some time. It came slowly and quietly to her window sill and peered into the kitchen. But it maintained a respectable distance from Kasturi and by not frightening her; it earned her respect and its first banana.

Those were the days of learning. Every day morning, Jup would sit on the kitchen window sill. It would observe her, making tea or using the cooker. It would observe Kasturi's ways of sweeping and swabbing the house. Of course, Jup had never known that something like tea or a cooker or a broom ever existed. Earlier, when it had lived with the little boy's family in Indonesia, it had been kept in an enclosure outside their house (in the garden). It had never been allowed to enter the little boy's home. It would be brought out only now and then to entertain human beings. It was in the little boy's home that Jup had seen the huge dust sucking monster for the first time. At that point of time, it did not know the name of the monster. But now, it knew that it was something that the humans called as a 'vacuum cleaner'.

*Like an apprentice, Jup learnt many things. He learnt that people don't like those, who talk too much. People don't like talking too little. Some people are good. Some others are wicked. Some understand and some others are not. Some people live with convictions. Some others live in confusion. For some, life is taken for granted. For others, life itself is a grant. He also learnt that those who worked hard are loved more.*

One day, Kasturi caught Jup in a net, which had been used earlier to trap wild animals and took him with her to Preetha's home. Preetha had built a lovely house on the banks of a beautiful little river. There was plenty of flora in and around her bungalow. The whole ambience reminded Jup of his home in Indonesia. The warmth of the surroundings warmed Jup's heart. The grey sky, the loveliness of the greenery, the wild flowers and fruits, the tingling fresh air and the clean mud welcome Jup. Although it had been captured in an unfriendly way, there was a sense of relief in Jup.

*'Will I find someone, who would be kind to me? Will I be able to find a kind master? Will there be someone to take care of me? Will I be of some use to my master? Is there any possibility of me going home to Saran in Indonesia? Even if I go back, will I be in a position to adjust to old ways?' wondered Jup.*

Kasturi knocked loudly on Preetha's door. Jnankeshwara opened the door and then, he and Shree Jay brought two chairs, one for Kasturi and one for Jup. Kastoori gave the orangutan, a new name; Pong. Kasturi and Pong waited patiently for Preetha. As soon as Preetha woke up, she rushed forward to meet her bosom friend, Kasturi.

Preetha began speaking, 'This morning, I was feeling very dull. Nothing interesting seemed to be happening. I had no meetings today and was not in a mood to write either. I was daydreaming and I visualized you coming to meet me and what a surprise!' Just then, Preetha noticed the orangutan. 'Well, I see you have brought a new friend to meet me.' Kasturi said, 'This monkey had settled in my garden and kept a watch on me. I used to observe it very carefully. It doesn't seem to belong to our land. Look at its complexion. It is almost orange! I thought of turning it over to the authorities but he looked friendly and I thought that I should show you, my new neighbour.'

Preetha coaxingly said, 'Come here, my dear. Now what's its name?'

Kasturi said, 'Pong.'

Preetha said, 'What a sweet name,' and smiled.

The monkey played with Preetha and somehow liked her. 'I have found my home,' thought Jup.

After all the conversation was over and cups of tea had been drunk, Kasturi decided to take leave.

'Preetha, I hope to meet you soon. Come, monkey come.'

The monkey did not budge. After patiently trying to pull Pong outside, Kasturi lost hope. 'It has become very stubborn like you, Kasturi,' said Preetha.

Kasturi replied, 'Preetha, I leave this monkey in your care.'

Preetha said, 'All right. I will take care of it, for the time being.'

The **time being** became a lifetime. From then on, the orangutan sitting in the first row of the audience in all her meetings was to floor them. It learnt to sit straight, in rapt attention, unlike some of the human counterparts, who endlessly scratched their heads, tapped their feet and stretched themselves or their feet... It became her avid fan, one who would read her books and observe the joyful glee on Preetha's face when she would finish writing them, each one of them. If it were to be asked as to where it had learnt English, it could be that its former little master had always spoken in English and Jup was always reading from his books. Pong soon learnt to make excellent tea in the traditional Indian style. It learnt to prepare special tea by adding powdered almonds and cardamoms in the concoction. It also helped Preetha in cooking. It learnt to keep a watch over the cooker. It would put the stopper on the cooker as and when the first whistle would come, reduce the flame on the second whistle and would then switch it off after three minutes. It learnt to note the time too.

Impressed with the intelligence displayed, Preetha purchased a watch and presented it to her pet. She tried to prevent Pong from working but soon realized that Pong was doing all the work, wantonly. It was clear that it loved working and it was doing it all out of affection. Thus, Pong became her travelling companion, avid fan, assistant and friend. Preetha lavished her loved pet with bananas, berries, sweets and mangoes.

The orangutan always slept on the floor. Preetha tried to coax it to sleep on the branches of their backyard tree but it refused. It had forgotten its earlier ways of living – since it had adopted a new human lifestyle and was now, afraid of falling! Preetha and Shree Jay prepared a warm bed under the Jackfruit tree for Pong with hardwood and hard work. For the first time, in several years, Pong or our Jup slept in peace.

# CHAPTER

## *Thirteen*

## Vijay Biswas

Vijay Biswas was a seasoned soul. He had worked very hard and had risen up to be one of the best inventors as well as physicians in the country. He was also a love poet and philosopher. A series of love failures had turned him into a love poet. Life had taught him that True intellect was in being wise. One day, he wrote the following poem.

> 'I am here,
> But I am elsewhere.
> The past is a dream,
> Shall I kill it?
> Each one chasing the other,
> We cannot remember every moment,
> Some shining, some submerge,
> Into our subconscious,
> I am here.
> The past is clear and

*Blurred,*

*But,*

*When our past dies,*

*We die,*

*When it lives,*

*We live,*

*I cannot kill my past,*

*For **the future** is the grandchild of the past.'*

# *Fourteen*

## *Kasturi's Sickness*

Shree Jay was a person, who was easily swayed by the parameters of any given situation. One day, Preetha asked him, 'Jay, do you have any wish, which I can fulfill? I have been able to fulfill the desires of several people with whom I share a relationship. I have now known you for long. It would be very fulfilling for me to have any desire of yours fulfilled.'

Shree Jay replied, 'If I have any such desire, Madam, I will straightaway bring it to your notice.'

*Of course, no man is without desire. Is a saint free from ambition? Shree Jay was a man who loved money and he found that the generous wage that he was receiving from Preetha was inadequate to satisfy his other unwarranted expenses.*

Actually, Shree Jay had wanted a pay raise. But somehow, he could not bring himself to asking Preetha for it. Slowly, Shree Jay started getting addicted to some vicious habits. Slowly, his need for a guaranteed supply of cash grew and he began to steal petrol from his owner's car. With time, this trick became quite regular. 'After all, what can I do? I need money,' thought Shree. He climbed the criminal learning ladder quickly and passed every theft activity with flying colours. Car parts were his next big discovery and he learnt to remove nuts, bolts and other parts of the car. Only a good memory reinforces both gratitude and guilt. Every time, Jay voluntarily forgot all his bad karma. Soon, Jay was no more afraid of committing any wrong.

One day, Preetha found out about the fraudulent practices of Shree Jay. Preetha Shri asked him to leave immediately and was never be seen by her again. Her former trusted friend and chauffeur from Gola Gampha was gone.

All these unhappy events were distressing to Preetha. She decided to visit her friend, Kasturi. Preetha made a trip to Kasturi's place. Kasturi welcomed her dear friend. Both were alike - ambiverts to the core. Their talks were always interesting and their ideas always agglutinated well and this usually led to the ascertainment of facts and helped both of them to reach correct conclusions.

Kasturi and Preetha began to discuss certain recent events - when all at once, Kasturi began sweating all over. Kasturi seemed terribly perturbed about something. Preetha Shree immediately demanded an explanation.

Kasturi said haltingly, 'I do not know. It's got something and to do with my coordination. I suddenly have fits of this type. 'Don't know!'

Kasturi was stammering violently. After some time, Kasturi recovered. She came near Preetha and embraced her. 'There is this sense of fear in me; some kind of phobia. I don't know. I feel like I am walking into darkness. Music no longer interests me. I feel like I have no connection with the world.'

Soon, Kasturi was trembling again. Preetha helped her on to the bed and prepared some tea. Jup aided her and carried the sunflower porcelain cup with the sweet tea for Kasturi. Kasturi was in utmost pain. She felt depressed and felt an invisible power pulling her down. It was like an evil power was dragging her into its dark shadows. She turned from one side to another and then the pain subsided in her sleep. It was clear to Preetha that her friend needed care and that she would have to maintain a balance between her existing writing obligations and her obligations to her friend. Her spirits tilted towards the latter with greater effect. She thought to herself, 'Moved no longer, By aubades or serenades, The soul's ear bends to hear, The distress in aggrieved hearts... Hands crave not to touch the lover, But to wipe the sufferers' tears...'

Several inexplicable fears had seized Kasturi. She took to long walks at all times during the day as well as during the night. All types of questions rose in her mind and perplexed it.

'I am going to die. What have I lived for and what should I live for? I have helped so many women to rehabilitate but all have turned out to be ungrateful.

Life is full of pain,' thought Kasturi. This was the second time that Kasturi was falling seriously ill. Shree Jay had saved her last time.

*'Will we ever come to a stage when only virtue prevails on the earth? If vice disappears, will virtue prevail? Where is God? Is pleasure the end of pain or is it the beginning? Is death, an end to life or a reaffirmation of life? Should one be a leader or a follower or a rebel who sets his own standards? What is religion? How absolute is one's existence? What is permanence? What is transience? What is love? What is fear? Yes, People become conscious of the real meaning of their lives only when they begin to suffer,' thought Kasturi.*

Thus, Kasturi was plagued by all kinds of various doubts and fears. Kasturi found it very difficult to answer these questions and of course, she couldn't answer them all. Nobody could answer her questions.

Preetha told her, after hearing her fears. 'Listen, Kasturi. You must not let your fears overcome you. Nobody can answer such questions. You are trying to study epiphenomena. It is quite useless - very futile to try to answer these questions. Your life is precious. You can be a mentor to many people!'

Preetha took care of all the needs of Kasturi including the task of preparing her meals. She hovered around her and took care of her more like an indulgent mother than like a friend. Her love was absolute. This was Preetha's way of repaying Kasturi's many acts of kindness. This unexpected break from her writing obligations was very beneficial for Preetha's health.

Kasturi's fears of not being able to answer all the questions of the world got diluted with time. She slowly came back to a somewhat normal state but this normality that she was experiencing was far from the normality of her earlier experiences. Kasturi was slowly realizing that the material phenomena were all false.

Though Kasturi no longer felt enslaved, she did not feel free either. She realized that man is very ordinary in an eternal world of the mystic cosmos. 'Man is vulnerable. Nature, fate, the future and the unknown are supreme. Man is only a scientist and not a supreme soul or an original creator.' The questions, which had arisen in the soul, seemed to ridicule the material world. She no longer had faith in the happenings of the world. She withdrew herself into a shell and hid herself. Kasturi composed a little song in her mind. The lines were very lyrical and went about like this....

> *'The earth was beginning to evolve,*
> *A new puzzle to be solved,*
> *Darkness had gone,*
> *A little carbon atom was born.*

> *The atom moved freely,*
> *From place to place,*
> *Healthy but not happy,*
> *As it traveled from place to place*
> *Little carbon felt useless,*
> *It felt tantamount to nothingness,*

*It felt tawdry,*
*And became moody.*
*An exasperated maker,*
*Made it into a gas,*
*He was not a forsaker,*
*He christened it 'Max'*
*Chemicals aggregated,*
*It became elated,*
*It felt stronger,*
*But still knew fear.*

*It cried and threw a tantrum,*
*It wept and wept,*
*The maker heard then,*
*And towards Man, he crept.*

*'What pains you asked he,*
*Max's reply made the maker laugh,*
*'You want to have a form like fish,*
*So you shall become fish.'*

*A million years flew by,*
*But the fish had not changed,*
*When the maker in his golden chariot*
*Was passing by,*
*He did not find in it, any change.*

*God again questioned Max,*
*Max said, it felt too taxed,*
*Swimming all day in cold water,*
*It wanted to become a walker.*
*Max became ape,*
*Then it became man,*
*One day, at night, he gaped,*
*At the glittering galaxy.*
*The vastness of the universe*
*Perturbed him,*
*Amazed him and reminded him,*
*Man was humbled,*
*On the truth, he had stumbled,*
***Life is what you make out of it.***

*He was still an atom,*
*Only bigger, wiser,*
*Yet a minute speck,*
*In the glittering galaxy.*
*The maker smiled and blessed him,*
*'May man remain the master.'*

Kasturi felt grateful to have Preetha for helping her to overcome her enormous mental strain. Preetha had been like a mother to her. Kasturi was very proud of her friendship with Preetha, which she believed was the greatest blessing of her life.

Thus, Kasturi suffered repeated nervous breakdowns. She became a recluse. It was a partly self-imposed exile and the rest was due to societal compulsions. The servants stopped coming as the manservant and the maids were beginning to feel afraid of the mood swings of their mistress. Slowly, Kasturi began to perform household chores, one by one with assistance being provided by Jup and Preetha.

Kasturi was soon diagnosed to be suffering from a deadly nervous disorder. Allopathic treatment proved futile. Soon, Kasturi's hopes subsided and were replaced by tsunami-sized doubts about her future.

Kasturi began walking around like a ghost. 'I don't have to forget my past for it has been highly creditable. Though this problem might have sent me out of action for the time being, my past can never be wiped out or demolished. I know no fear now,' reassured Kasturi to herself. Kasturi was now malleable and very vulnerable. The tough shell had been broken - exposing the soft inner self.

Preetha said, 'Yes and you need not worry. We can combat the world together. I shall leave Jup with you to give you company. You will need company. I will rush back to you in a few weeks after completing a few professional obligations.'

Preetha did not want Kasturi to feel distressed or excluded. She knew that patients require care, compassion and companionship above anything else. It would be necessary to provide monetary, material, moral, and service support to Kasturi and Preetha knew about her duties and wished to discharge them to the best of her ability and beyond it. Preetha knew that her small but consistent endeavours would lead up to huge success.

Meanwhile, Victor and his wife, Mala who were regular visitors to Preetha's residence noted her sudden disappearances with despair. Of course, nobody thought of complaining to the police because they were all quite aware of Preetha's queer ways of accomplishing various tasks. When Victor came to know about Preetha's return, he straightaway headed towards her home and it was the great expectation of meeting her that made him to smile a bit too often during the hour's trip in his car. His chauffeur wondered if he had done anything clumsy. 'It's none of my business, anyway to study the moods of my boss,' thought Victor's chauffeur.

The moment Victor saw Preetha, he felt greatly reassured and chastened. 'What happened to you? You are queerer than ever,' said Victor to Preetha in a matter-of –fact, 'I know it all' tone. He continued after a slight pause. 'We all love you because of your queerness.'

Preetha told him about Kasturi.

Preetha said, 'I just don't know what to do. I just can't bear to see her like this - so sick and vulnerable! She used to be so self-assured and now she needs a prop. These men of medicine spend half their lives studying the subject and now they are saying that there is no cure! Victor, let me tell you that human beings are not born to suffer! No cure, says this doctor!!' There was a sense of disbelief in her as she uttered the words.

Victor said, 'I totally disagree with you. There is no real suffering. Man has created sufferings for himself. Man has been born to enjoy the gifts of nature. Have you heard about Vijay? He is my friend. He has solutions for every problem!'

Preetha said, 'Bishwas? The genius inventor and physician! Absolutely! Who would not know him? He is a dynamic personality but I hear that he is actually a depressed soul. The manipulations of the media! The manipulations of the man! Whatever the truth, I have great respect for the man for his superior knowledge. His intellectualism is our country's gift. His disposition really endears him to all the people. Indeed, who would not love to be as famous as him? Now, what about him?'

Victor said, 'Don't be jealous! You are very famous yourself!'

Preetha said, 'Perhaps! Now, what is that you wanted to say about him?'

Victor said, 'You seem to have a huge stock of opinion about Biswas. He can help Kasturi. That is what I believe. When can Biswas and I come to meet you? I am sure that he will be able to save Kasturi.'

Preetha said, 'Anytime!' She continued, 'Victor, Why do you pretend as though I am one of those cruel people, who give an appointment after a lot of harassment? Victor just smiled and said, 'Thursday noon is a good time to meet. We will see you, then.'

Preetha said, 'Everyday is a good day for good people. You are welcome at all times. I have never considered you as a mere friend, Victor and you know that very well. You are a part of my family. Of course, Shree Jay was a part of my extended family, too. I always considered him as a son but he turned out to be tremendous failure and the young lad has lost his place. I hope at least you, Pong, Kasturi and Mala will remain with me. Jnankeshwara remains my most faithful disciple, as yet.' Her soft voice then added, 'I really hope.'

Jnankeshwara (who was sitting in a corner of the room) heard this comment, while proof reading Preetha's manuscripts. His face was expressionless. He continued his work.

Jnankeshwara said, 'Mother, I have finished proof reading. Dinner is ready. Please come.' Jnankeshwara had his meal a little later after the duo had finished theirs. Victor went his way. Preetha was looking deeply sorrowful. Her worries engulfed her. They were about Kasturi. She felt as if all her friends were in trouble.

She asked, 'Jnan, how long are you going to remain with me?'

Jnan replied, 'As long as my soul rests in my body.'

Preetha asked, 'Have you seen your soul?'

Jnan replied, 'No, I haven't.'

Preetha asked, 'How are you so sure?'

Jnan replied, 'Souls are invisible.'

Preetha said, 'Of course. Jnan, would you like to get married?'

Jnan said, 'Of course not.'

Jnan thought, 'Of course, I wish to marry, but who will wish to marry me?' Preetha could sense his thoughts. Years of existence with a person make us know exactly what the other person is thinking. *Call it telepathy or reasoning*!

Preetha said, 'Don't worry, I already know.'

Jnan was bewildered. He could not understand as to how Preetha could read his mind.

~ ~ ~

Kasturi was very exhausted. Her body was in pain, listening to the complaints of her neural connections. On the other side of the night, as it headed towards the morning, she woke up and her mind refused to be taken back into its earlier position of stupor. She found that Jup was peacefully sleeping on its warm bed on the floor. Jup had no fear. Sensing some shadow over it, Jup jumped.

Jup looked at his former mistress, Kasturi. Jup did not notice in Kasturi, any disorder. It was as affectionate as ever. Being just an animal and lacking the 'sixth sense', it was unable to discover in Kasturi, any disorder. It was affectionate as usual, pulling her hair every now and then like misbehaving child. Kasturi got up to prepare for herself, a steaming cup of coffee. 'Now, where is the coffee powder? Aha!' Kasturi looked at the hot and bubbling coffee decoction with glee. The just prepared coffee quickly descended down her food pipe. The effect was quite remarkable. Her spirits soared. She looked out through her room's window. She saw a head turn in her direction. The face in the head showed repulsion and the steps related to that head quickly moved away. Her spirit nose-dived. She felt waves of hatred rise within her.

A few days later, Victor came with Vijay to meet Preetha. Vijay had mixed feelings when he entered Preetha's house. There were a number of bewitching paintings on the wall. Their beauty struck him but there were just too many of them, everywhere. Every wall was cluttered with colours.

Vijay remarked, 'Ah! These lovely colours have captured my heart.' He then thought to himself –'She must be a full-blown megalomaniac.'

Preetha interrupted his stream of thoughts by saying, 'Hello! Hello! Mr. Bishwas. Welcome to my house!'

Just then Victor came from behind and in a bellowing voice said, 'Hello! Mala had some work to be completed. So, I left her behind. I want you to meet Bishwas, my friend. He also happens to be my fan. One day, I saw him frantically making a beelike towards me, during a shooting. I was full of pride and proceeded in the direction of friendship with this wonderful man. I heard his appreciation with pleasure. He was totally unassuming and I was such a goat! It was much later that I realized about his prominence from a co-artiste.'

Bishwas had only shy smile lighting up his square countenance, for these words. Vijay said, 'You have been quite lavish in your appreciation. Thank you.'

Victor said, 'Now, coming to the point, Preetha has a problem and I am sure Vijay has a very strong chance of being able to solve it.'

After hearing Preetha's elucidation, Bishwas spoke, 'Well, I have just made a concoction. It is still under experimentation. Since your friend's deadly skin problem has been given up as being incurable, I could give it a try, but of course, the results are unpredictable. It could worsen her condition. It will require a long treatment with herbs, aromas, colours and punctures. I will have to be near her at all times, night and day to observe any minute change.' Preetha said, 'Mr. Bishwas, I beseech you to help my friend. If I were a scientist, I could have helped her but unfortunately, my knowledge about the concerned subject is less. Perseverance is one thing and knowledge of certain subjects is another and I am very confident that if you will pursue your goal with intense perseverance, success will be yours.'

Bishwas said, 'There are times when the question is not one of persistence, but of faith, not in ones' capacity but in the superior power, which governs our life; call it karma or God.'

~ ~ ~

Around this period, a woman called Sathyavahini was jobless. She was in a despondent state. Of what use to her was her good character? Nobody was prepared to help her. She was in a situation wherein only poverty was willing to take her in. She was willing to take up any job. She found work at Preetha's place and became her chauffeur. It was quite strange for an educated person like Sathyavahini to take up such a profession but any honourable job was at the moment, most welcome to her. Sathyavahini was both peaceful and dignified. Jnan simply hated the sight of Preetha being so friendly with Sathya. He tried poisoning Preetha's ears with complaints against the new worker but Preetha being intelligent knew the distinction between reality and falsehood. Jnan suffered, whenever he saw Sathyavahini and Preetha's increasing dependence on the former. Jnankeshwara waited with patience for the first false step of his opponent. Sathyavahini for her part had this deep respect for Jnan for his loyalty to Preetha, his goodness and his culinary abilities. She also loved him for his big sad bulging eyes, which were glazed with a strange determination in them. She saw in him, a strange simplicity, which she had not noticed in any other man.

Jnankeshwara made all kinds of allegations against Sathyavahini. He slowly poisoned Preetha's ears with dirty stuff about the new helper. Meanwhile Preetha had developed, the highest opinion of the pretty young girl.

One day, Preetha asked Sathyavahini, 'Don't you think it is time to marry?'

Sathyavahini replied, 'A little later.'

Preetha asked, 'What about now?'

Sathyavahini replied, 'Now is never the moment.'

Preetha said, 'But you must'

Sathyavahini, 'If you instruct.'

Preetha said, 'I do.'

Sathyavahini said, 'I accept but who, may I ask, is the person in question?'

Preetha said, 'Jnankeshwara'. Sathyavahini felt an enormous burden being lifted off her heart. Her life was almost settled. She now had a job and soon, she would be married, too. When Jnankeshwara was instructed by Preetha to marry Sathya, he too decided to give up his unethical ways of tormenting Sathya. He too experienced a similar kind of relief, freed from the delusions of jealousy and hatred.

After the ceremony, Preetha said, 'The most enduring are the most faithfully rewarded.' Preetha mischievously smiled.

# CHAPTER

## Fifteen

## *Kasturi's Love*

Taking Preetha's request to heart, Vijay pulled his spirit, mind and body together in his new mission to combat the disease, which had afflicted Kasturi. He didn't know as to how long it would take for him to achieve tangible results.

Bishwas announced to Kasturi. 'My name is Bishwas. Preetha must have informed you, prior to my coming.'

Kasturi said, 'Hello, Bishwas. I have heard a lot about you from Preetha.' There was sorrow dripping in her voice. 'Come in.'

Bishwas entered her house and saw Jup darting over the curtains. The new guest got a simian welcome with Jup jumping up and down saying, 'Chee, chee, chee,' barring its yellow tainted teeth. Jup was more quiet than usual.

Preetha had come with Bishwas. Preetha was standing behind him. His huge proportions hid hers.

Kasturi had not yet noticed her. Distress had affected Kasturi's perceptions very adversely. Preetha was perturbed at her friend's state and did not wish to remain in such circumstances as to disturb her friend. Preetha took a turn and climbed on to her waiting car and asked Sathyavahini to drive her home. All that needed to be communicated to Biswas had already been communicated to him.

Initially, Kasturi was informed by her new doctor about his plan to treat her. She was to begin his treatment, which would last several months. The treatment was to be on a day-to-day basis. He soon occupied a residence, a few blocks away from where she lived.

Bishwas said, 'Don't worry. You will soon be totally fit and fine. You need not show, any worry or fear as both are only trying to perpetuate themselves in you. We will not let our enemies succeed.'

Kasturi was surprised that a man of such intellectualism and beauty could look at her unhealthy conditions with so much kindness. 'This man is nice. He does not put on airs,' thought Kasturi. The slow and steady voice of Biswas had a therapeutic effect on Kasturi. Kasturi said, 'Thank you very much indeed.'

Bishwas stayed close to Kasturi's house. He took wonderful care of her as a doctor. He systematically addressed her problem with medicines for her body and kind words for her soul. He told her to take his medicines on time. Of course, he did fear that the medicines that he had prescribed for her might not work in the way he desired. 'What if it were to aggravate her problem?' thought Biswas.

The problem shifted from the skin to the mind. He quickly withdrew the medicines on time and her mind recovered its state of tranquillity. In spite of what she had been through, Kasturi retained her trust in Bishwas. She constantly thought, 'Bishwas is going to cure me. I am going to be just perfect as I was and much better.' Soon after, Bishwas decided to shift his course of treatment to the exclusive use of herbs. Kasturi's response to herbs was truly excellent. Her hopes of recovery reached new crests and unknown to her, the reason for the hope was to never reach its trough. It didn't happen overnight. It took time but the cure was unquestionable. Kasturi was truly happy and thanked her saviour, Bishwas, again and again repeatedly and in earnest. She was full of love for him and looked forward to expressing the same for him. Earlier, her skin had turned to a point where it could no longer dictate terms to its owner or the one who could so radically manoeuvre its feelings. However now, the spots lightened and the skin began to show symptoms of regaining its lost glow.

Soon, Kasturi developed a deep desire to marry Bishwas and she saw no barriers to her desire to marry Bishwas. Of course, her judgement was not totally accurate, for she could only understand herself and not the person at the other end. Bishwas was mentally unprepared for what he was to hear from her. Being wounded by womanhood once, he did not have too much strength to face any woman. Unknown to Kasturi, there was another thought and another feeling which had guided him in his desire to help Kasturi in more ways than one.

There was this one thought which had pulled him to do what he had done to cure Kasturi. 'Initially, Preetha had seemed to be a megalomaniac but isn't one really. She has been such a perfect friend to Kasturi. She has supported one with such an abominable skin and mental illness. Preetha is compassionate and loving. Preetha has many virtues and few vices and she is good. She is good enough for me. Her virtues eclipse her vices and it is true that fame does affect people, a bit. It wouldn't take too much of an effort to love her. Yes, I just need to have the patience to put things in the right perspective.'

To put it simply, Bishwas' affection for Kasturi whom he regarded as a sister was a mere offshoot of his love for someone else he desired to marry. Kasturi, at this point, opened the issue before him but Bishwas did not oblige her. Preetha seemed to fit his requirements. She was both good and intelligent. Kasturi felt like a wounded lioness. It angered her that her beauty had been unable to elicit the response that she had hoped it would. She sought revenge and waited patiently for an opportunity to strike back. Soon, Kasturi got back her lost health, beauty and lustre- thanks to the effective medicines of Dr.Biswas.

Preetha felt very elated on hearing that Kasturi had recovered and that she was healthy. Kasturi had recovered but only physically. The pangs of jealousy and anger had devastated Kasturi.

One day, Preetha came to meet her friend and said, 'Hello, Kasturi. I am very happy. This is the happiest day of my life.' Kasturi embraced her and thought something sinister and then said, 'Yes.'

# CHAPTER

## *Sixteen*

## *Vijay and Preetha*

Though Kasturi was genuinely grateful to Preetha, for all that she had done, there was a dual nature to her feelings. There were bursts of anger, followed by pangs of guilt, followed by acts of goodness and good words, which were again followed by bursts of anger. This followed endlessly. Preetha was quite surprised at this display of weird behaviour on behalf of her friend. She could not understand it.

*Actually, Kasturi was jealous of Preetha.* Preetha's personal and professional success was consuming her. Preetha was not aware of the diabolical nature of Kasturi and loved the latter without realising Kasturi's true intentions. Meanwhile, Bishwas proposed to Preetha but Preetha rejected him outright. In fact, she was not interested in marriage. She wanted to retain her independence. *She was to learn that true freedom and independence lies in a certain degree of bondage.*

One day, Preetha had some urgent work and had to leave her office, all at once. Finally, Kasturi had got the opportunity that she was hoping for. She stealthily entered Preetha's room and threw one by one, all of Preetha's literary creations into the fire- place. The fire burnt all the papers and also her anger. Moments later, Kasturi was filled with remorse but she also desired to hide her guilty act. She knew that what she had done was wrong but she had reached a stage when by exposing herself, she would only be led to further exclusion and would lose a very good friendship. When Preetha returned home, she became shocked on hearing about the outbreak of fire in her chamber. She didn't suspect Kasturi but nevertheless asked Kasturi as to where she was, when the accident happened. Kasturi denied going into Preetha's room that morning.

*Kasturi's friendship with Preetha survived and Kasturi gave up wanting to marry Vijay. Suddenly, friendship seemed more reliable than love.*

Mr. Rajas Kumar was Kasturi's neighbour. He had moved in recently. He found Kasturi to be a most interesting girl, who was very bold and sweetly stubborn. He believed in the art of persuasion and he was an insurance agent. One day, he finally talked to Kasturi.

Kasturi said, 'Your powers of persuasion will not overwhelm me and let me tell you, I hate men. I have already been deceived, once.'

Rajas said, 'I don't hate women. I respect women. I am especially very fascinated by your anger and your stubbornness. I know that you will find it strange but your vices attract me more than your virtues. Of course, you have achieved a lot, too.'

Kasturi said, 'Don't you understand? I hate men. You must have read my research findings.'

Rajas said, 'All men are not bad. There must be exceptions.'

Kasturi said, 'Let me ask you a question? Now, how will you impress upon me that you are faithful and understanding?'

Rajas Kumar replied, 'Marry me. To know the value of something, you must first experience it.' Kasturi said, 'I don't believe in the institution.

Finally, she did and she married Rajas Kumar.

~ ~ ~

Jnankeshwara, however, did not desire that Preetha remain alone. He wanted to curb her independence and he plotted with Sathyavahini to accomplish his goal of forcing Preetha into marrying Vijay Biswas for by now, the duo them had by now understood the infinite value of the kind man. In addition, Bishwas was on his way up the ladder of meritorious distinctions in the medical profession. Success breeds success but in the case of Biswas, success was also breeding jealousy.

Jnankeshwara and Sathyavahini insisted that Preetha marry Bishwas and settle in life. She was reaching middle age, now. 'It is your final chance to enter into an alliance,' said Jnan to Preetha, one day.

Preetha replied, 'I prefer to remain like a solitary coconut tree than a clump of bushes. I wish to faithfully serve the society with my offerings. I detest any change in my routine. I wish to be of utility to everyone. I do not wish to be a burden. No man can change my will. I will remain as independent as I wish to be. I am an independent army.'

Jnankeshwara efforts were thwarted but not for long.

~ ~ ~

*Preetha was not an ordinary person to be disheartened by failures. She had great faith in her skills. She kept working hard and improved her writing prowess. She earned more and helped more people. She began to have an impact on people's lives. More and more pages bled out of her pen, in earnest. 'In order to attain true success and permanent joy in life, one would have to overcome life's lamentations,' thought Preetha and she didn't lose hope and it was therefore, unsurprising that both fame and wealth had begun to shower upon Preetha. She wrote with renewed faith in herself. She had come to know that that the secret of success was pain. Slowly but surely, Preetha was becoming like a Samurai Sword. She had been subject to multiple fires of life, repeatedly and had emerged as a Fiery Woman. She had become a very strong personality. There were so many people, who had burnt her - the ones she had trusted as her own family and friends and yet, she had emerged from the ashes.*

# SECTION
## *Two*

## *Karma Theory
(The Rebirth)*

*Nothing in this world happens by accident. Every reaction in this world has had its beginning in some other action committed in perhaps, another time and in another place and perhaps, by some other person. There is an inexplicable and remarkable continuity in life both on the physical and metaphysical realm.*

*Human beings have always been in the pursuit of different ends to realize their desires. Many have traversed the human plains and gained but what exactly have they gained? Some of us gain wealth, some gain happiness, some gain peace, some gain health and some gain, a combination of all these wonderful gems of life. Everyone is desirous of gaining greater and greater insights about the world. All of us make a beginning, move further on in our paths and reach different destinations experiencing variegated and myriad emotions as well as situations. Surprisingly, it can be noted that the very same experiences elicit different responses in different people in different times. The beginning of all of this lies in the cognitive process, which is often itself influenced by external circumstances.*

*The most difficult task to do in the world is thinking. Some people make a living out of thinking. They are the great day dreamers. These great day dreamers are those, who present us with the widest of choices in arts and sciences of all kinds: literature, music, dance, drama, theatre, drawing and painting, sculpting, mathematics and scientific progress.*

*Each one of us in life, who is born wants to achieve some success in life and even if that success may not always be a part of our immediate realty, it is not in human nature to give up easily, as essentially a huge part of our human life is trying to find out where we fit in the big picture. Essentially, each of us is trying to find out about our Karma. People like Tesla, Newton, Einstein, Darwin, Bose, Gandhi and Curie have all had a great role to play in trying to help lesser mortals reach the goal of Truth.*

*There is nothing new in this world. After all, energy cannot be created or destroyed but merely takes different forms.* **Preetha is reborn as Ganga.** *It is year 2016. India had attained independence in 1947. India was now a free nation. The land of palaces, history, natural beauty, Information Technology and techies was also the land of Shri Ram, The Buddha, The Mahavira and Guru Nanak as well as leaders like Gandhi, Modi and Jayalalithaa.*

# CHAPTER

## Seventeen

## Ganga

*'There is permanence,*
*Within transience,*
*The joy in attaining an object,*
*The pain in parting with the subject,*
*In both is our time lost,*
*It leaves an imprint like a dot,*
*Yet,*
*All remains forever,*
*In the memory,*
*Life's inventory,*
*Free, fresh and lasting.'*

'Ganga' was the name that her mother had given her. It was a very traditional Indian name. The river, Ganges has been celebrated throughout India and throughout the varying time frames of history. There has never been a river more famed nor revered than the Ganga in

India. The Ganga has been the ever-loving mother for millions of Indians who have always regarded the river as being holy. It has been fabled to bestow upon those who bathe in it with moksha or the freedom from the cycle of birth and death. The river, Ganga has always been the synonym of purity and it was for this very reason that Ganga's mother had named her so.

Ganga's family was rich and she was spoilt. They stayed on Ashoka Road, one of the few places in Delhi, which had a canopy of trees, especially Jamun trees. Ganga's favourite haunt was the Jamun tree in their garden. The tree bore rich juicy blackish blue fruits in the months of May, June and July, the hottest months in the capital of India, coinciding with the arrival of the south-east monsoons in the month of July. The days were passing quickly. Ganga was transitioning from school to college. This particular incident took place during Ganga's college vacation.

The day had started as usual. The vehicles were honking and ponking on the busy Ashoka Road. At seven in the morning, The paperwallah was screaming 'paper....paper' at the top of his voice. The honking and ponking of the vehicles on the road blended in an unruly way with the voice of the paper-wallah, who collected old newspapers. He had never forgotten his 7 o'clock morning routine for the past twenty years, which covered the major part of Ganga's existence on the earth. The traffic noise, inter-mingling with the voice of the paper-wallah seemed to happily welcome the sound of the screeching rickshaws plying on the roads. Inside Ganga's home, all these noises mixed incoherently with the sound of the working mixie-jar, which was grinding a south Indian traditional dish called 'idli' batter and the washing machine, which was going 'tting,tting tting' to indicate that the clothes were ready for putting up for drying. These head-splitting noises were a part of everyday humdrum. There was nothing to indicate that it would be an unusual day. Her mother had given her an important task to be completed and she had as usual, forgotten to do the work; lost as she was in her own lackadaisical world and that was it. The usual benevolence of the mother was lost to the emerging anger of the situation. This was followed by a voluble lecture by her mother on discipline and duty. She concluded her speech with the following words directed towards her daughter.

'What have you accomplished in your life? Have you ever done anything on your own without being dependent on either your father or me? Can you gain gold in a righteous way?' asked her mother, throwing an open challenge, in front of everyone.

Ganga replied nonchalantly, 'Yes, I can.'

Ganga's arrogant attitude irked her mother and she told her daughter, 'I challenge you to accomplish something on your own.'

For a minute, Ganga did not care about her mother's statement. But then, in the next few minutes, as her inner confidence woke her up, Ganga's mind began to concoct a new and adventurous idea. She decided to accept her mother's challenge. But right at that moment, she did not react.

That night as she slept, she had a strange vision like dream. She could see herself, looking at the experiences of someone else's life. She even felt as if she was someone else. She saw a human couple in the vision. She felt as if she knew them very well. The smile on the man's face seemed familiar. She could hear voices calling out. 'Preetha....Vijay...' She had seen this couple somewhere. In fact, she felt as if she had lived with them. It felt eerie and all this seemed to connect her to some unknown mysterious past. Ganga got up with a start and found sparkling round sweat-beads dotting the landscape of her forehead.

*Ganga was the rebirth of Preetha. Her soul was still evolving. It was just that she didn't know all this, yet!*

The following morning witnessed the assembling together of all the family members belonging to different age groups in the brahmasthanam or the central open space of their house. It was Ganga who had requested all of them to assemble.

'Let me travel throughout the length and breadth of India for one whole year. Give me some money and at the end of the year, I will come back to you after making considerable gains,' said Ganga to her astounded family members. Her family was sceptical about Ganga's challenge and initially, they took it to be some kind of a joke. Unbelievable stuff said on the spur of a moment is seldom considered valid but Ganga's seriousness made them realize the sincerity of her intentions. There was an element of disbelief in the entire situation. Her mother felt as if a bombshell had been dropped on her.

Two days later, much to everyone's surprise, Ganga was ready for her journey. Emotions were running high in Ganga's home. Ganga's mother was not in the best of spirits. She knew that her daughter had accepted her challenge. She also knew her daughter's adamant nature. She knew that she was responsible for all that was happening. Her daughter would go to any extent to win in her challenge. Her mother called her and told her, 'My child, I don't know if you must go but if you really want to go, then do travel and see our most blessed country; our country, which is the cradle of human civilization.'

Her mother continued to speak. 'It is the womb of some of the greatest religions of the world and it is the land where men belonging to different regions, religions and communities live in harmony, treating each other with respect and dignity. You must see its contours and its children and know how they live. There are good and evil elements everywhere. You must learn how to deal with both the categories. You will have to overcome all the obstacles in your path if you want to reach your goal and make some gain. For that, you will have to be strong and courageous. You must learn to do one thing properly at a time and you must know what to do and when. I advise you to engage yourself in excellent time management. Everything has a value only when it is done at the right time. You must equip yourself monetarily, for the world does not pity or help the poor. 'So, here, take this money', she said, handing over to Ganga, a lot of cash in a bag. 'I know you will say that it is a better idea to withdraw money using your ATM debit cards, which is a lot easier but then unless you do as I say, you will never know how difficult it is to keep your cash money safely, dear.' She continued, 'You might think that this is a lot of money but it isn't, for our country is bigger and more beautiful than what your powers of comprehension might tell you and you will need every paisa. So, learn to be watchful and careful. I suggest that you take our faithful dog, 'Benevolence', with you. It will be your guardian, friend and protect you like a brother.'

Ganga replied, 'Thank you, mother. I will take it with me.' 'Benevolence,' she said addressing her pet dog, 'I hope you are happy with my decision.' Benevolence barked to display its happiness for it was as eager to see India, as was its master, Ganga. Soon, Ganga found herself bidding farewell to her discombobulated family. She picked up her bags, her bundle of money and then the duo of master and pet animal left their home to disappear into the succeeding sequence of events. It was exactly 12.00 noon and the day was the 16th August, just one day after the Indian Independence Day was celebrated with gusto throughout India. The year was 2004 A.D.

Ganga began to walk slowly. Ganga remembered about how she had drawn a seven-card spread of tarot cards, just the week before. The focus card had been an upright 'The Fool', which meant folly and thoughtlessness. 'How true, the prediction was,' she thought. She could have as well as done the task that her mother had given her and not incurred her wrath. Ganga also remembered that her last card was the upright 'The World'. She would surely be able to attain her goal, successfully and return home with her dignity intact. Ganga wanted to return home, triumphantly.

'Here I am, a person with a confused mind making my way to the railway station to make some gain by the end of a journey to some unknown destination! What's happening?' she thought. She felt like crying like a child, which had just lost its favourite toy. She felt like going back home. But she successfully resisted the temptation. Her goal seemed very distant and home was very near.

'I am the master of my own destiny and here I am, at the helm of my own affairs. I have this wonderful opportunity before me that most people can only dream about. I must make the best use of this opportunity. I will not become frail but will seek strength. I will not go home without achieving something big,' thought Ganga, trying to take charge of herself.

She walked on. Change was something that Ganga had always detested. More than the changes itself, it was the speed of change that she abhorred. With sudden changes having made inroads into her life in a very impertinent manner; Ganga did not feel very convinced about what she had just done and was planning to do. She felt as if she needed some assurance from someone or something from somewhere and quickly.

On a sudden thought, Ganga opened up her bright and big pink purse and delved deep into its contents. She removed from it, a booklet on Indian tourism. She glanced at the cover and read the title, 'Incredible India'. *Indeed, it was all quite incredible, a woman on the streets of Delhi with this booklet in her insecure hands not knowing what to do or where to go! Yet, there was something fantastic about all this!*

Ganga read the address standing on a dusty Delhi pavement. She pulled out her mobile and dialed zero… one…one…two…three…three…two…zero…zero… zero…five. Someone on the other side of the line picked up and spoke, 'Yes. This is the India Tourism Delhi Office. May I help you?' The conversation between the two ended on a pleasant note. Ganga seemed a bit pleased and she patted Benevolence's soft and fluffy head. 'Well, well, what have we got ahead of us?' said Ganga to her four-legged faithful friend.

Ganga had been born and brought up in Delhi. Delhi seemed to be constantly changing and was a cauldron of variegated and interacting cultures. There had never been a period in the history of Delhi when it had not changed. Its contours were constantly changing and there were, very often, new appearances and disappearances, some as deceptive as some others were forthright. She had played, walked and spent all her precious hours in the city. She had never been to any other place. She had never imagined even in her dreams that Delh, which housed her home would provide the beginning to all the drama and action that would take place.

~ ~ ~

There were two Delhi's, the old Delhi with its minarets and forts and the New Delhi with its fast paced life, buildings, skyscrapers and Business Process Outsourcing Centres. Ganga had studied in one of the elite schools and had continued with her college education in an even more prestigious institution. Ganga wondered as to what her friends would have to say to her about her incredible tryst with destiny. Ganga quelled her imaginary ephemeral fears and convinced herself that she was capable of accomplishing what she had set out to do, which was to travel and see a vibrant India. She was also intelligent enough to understand that she would have to take care of herself without expecting emotional or material support from others.

'Delhi, the capital of this incredible and dashing India is the right place to begin my journey,' thought Ganga. Benevolence nodded its head and seemed to agree. 'Delhi has a long history full of marvels - the Qutub Minar, the Red Fort and the Jantar Mantar. A slave emperor had captured the most coveted and powerful throne of Delhi and had built the Qutub Minar. Delhi is full of many places filled with the fragrance of history but where should I start? Should I start from the Jantar Mantar, the astronomical observatory built by the great Raja Sawai Jai Singh or should I start my journey from The Jama Masjid with its minarets and dominating domes? Perhaps it would be a good decision to first visit the Red Fort, from where every year, our Prime Minister gives his Independence Day speech to our people,' thought Ganga still not very clear about what to do.

By this time, Ganga was feeling hungry and settled for the nearby South Indian restaurant. As she tried to walk into the restaurant with her dog, someone standing near the entrance told her that pets were not allowed on the premises. Benevolence had to wait outside the restaurant. Ganga sat on a chair next to the table nearest to the entrance. Ganga ordered a few south Indian dishes, which she shared with Benevolence. Sitting outside, Benevolence gleefully gobbled up the food while a shocked waiter looked on. Pets were not allowed but the restaurant couldn't risk losing a customer. The waiter felt repulsive towards the adorable and bouncy Benevolence the strange man never liked dogs!. At the same time, he was quite overawed by the beauty of its master. After paying the bill, Ganga and Benevolence left the restaurant.

As she stepped out of the restaurant, Ganga resolved to be more frugal. Money was a precious commodity, which would need to be her loyal friend throughout her adventure. Ganga was learning fast. 'People are kind but who would be generous enough to part with their money?' thought Ganga as she patted her conspicuous bag containing her bundle of money. She was learning quickly about the value of money. Wealth and pompousness, which had been the watchwords of Ganga's world, seemed to have lost their charm for Ganga. She was beginning to understand the struggles of the common people.

Just around those moments of contemplation, her cell phone rang. She picked it up and spoke, 'Hello! May I know who is speaking? Oh! Mom, it is you!' The reply on the other side seemed to never end. 'It is me, your mother. Ganga, I am really scared. I don't want you to go. I am serious. What are you going to gain? I am sorry that I hurt you but you must know better than trying to gain something by travelling to places unknown to you and that too, unaccompanied! Come back!' Ganga's mother began to cry profusely but her daughter had decided to be adamant and refused to budge. Ganga expressed a genuine desire to travel and to explore the vastness of her country and to learn from the experiences from her travel. Finally, without compromising on her dignity by shedding tears or begging for favours, Ganga managed to convince her mother about her desire to explore her country.

Ganga told her mother- 'Mother, henceforth, my phone will always remain switched on till I come back. You can speak to me whenever you want. Nevertheless, I request you to remain calm and to call me up only from time to time. I may be going to places lost by man to the ravages of time. I will return with some substantial gain. I will be successful. You must not contact me often. I will gain. I will gain.'

Instead of going to the Red Fort as had been planned earlier, Ganga took the Delhi Transport Corporation bus to the Bahai House of Worship. As soon as she got down from the Delhi public bus, she walked up to the lotus-shaped marble temple and stood before it. She prayed silently to the Gods to break her resolve to travel alone and to send her scurrying back home to her parents! Yet, she felt, a contradictory and powerful wave of intuition asking her to stay back and to continue her journey.

The renaissance of an underlying thought made her to decide to visit the edicts of the king Ashoka. She took a rugged ride on one of the city's many autorickshaws (on her way saw some very poor people without even proper clothing and felt very sad about it) and reached the place, where the edicts of Ashoka, the Great stood. Ganga had always been interested in history for she was a strong believer in the theory that there is no present or future without a past. 'Ashoka was one of the greatest kings of India who had renounced war and had taken to the path of Dharma as had been advocated by the Buddha, the Light of Asia, after the Kalinga war which left thousands, dead and injured. The Buddha had become the Buddha after seeing the four great signs; the old man, the diseased man, the dead man and the monk. Had Buddha been alive, he would have been unhappy to see the newer fifth sign; the poor and despondent. God did not create poverty but men for vested interests have managed to perpetuate poverty,' thought Ganga as she reflected upon the scenes of poverty that she had come across.

The place where Ganga stood was full of many five star hotels. There were also wretched beggars, all around the place. 'Of what use is all this prosperity if poverty cannot be made impoverished?' thought Ganga. The unexplored India, which she had never known, when she was part of it was slowly acquiring larger than life qualities as her journey seemed to opening up an incredible cauldron of contradictions in life.

Ganga decided to move on, leaving behind her thoughts. She travelled up to Daryaganj in the northern part of the city to buy a radio cum tape recorder. She was able to obtain one at Daryaganj at the price of just two hundred. Well, it was second-hand but its songs were blazingly clear. Ganga knew that she had been able to purchase happiness for a mere two hundred. She loved listening to old Hindi songs. This radio-cum-tape recorder along with 'Benevolence' would remain her companions. At no 88, Janpath road, at the India Tourism Office, she picked up some more information to facilitate her forthcoming journeys. India beckoned Ganga and was beginning to seduce her. Ganga was slowly realizing that India was a ravishingly beautiful country but that it was not without burdens. Ganga was blissfully unaware of the adventures that she would be a part of in the forthcoming events of her life. Would she gain something or would she return with tears in her eyes, to her parents regretting her decision to see India, her country? What would she gain and how? Would the world in India meet Ganga's expectations or would they be throttled? Could Ganga gain and gather something special?

Ganga soon boarded a train to Jaipur in Rajasthan. Ganga looked at the changing landscape in awe.

# CHAPTER
## *Eighteen*
## Understanding

How different, Delhi seemed from the window of an Indian train! The dark and dull colours of the New Delhi landscape - the moody moulds, the blistering buildings, the chattering crowds, the bargaining bazaars and the terrifying traffic had been left behind and were slowly giving way for the sands of the state of Rajasthan. Ganga was soon feeling bored and hungry. She made Benevolence sit next to her bag and expected it to watch over her money. Ganga walked up to the cafeteria on her train to buy some noodles.

When she returned, she found her Benevolence looking with wonder, with its mildly dilated curiously beautiful eyes - at the orange sun kissing the sky rehearsing for the arrival of a perfectly nonchalant twilight as if it were a prelude to the masked night! Just then her eyes drifted to the space where her bag should have been. Her bag containing her bundle of money was nowhere to be seen. In panic, she asked her co-passenger, 'Did you see my bag? It is a big one, white in colour with a purple design on it.' Her co-passenger, a tough looking old man replied in the negative. Ganga was beginning to feel distraught, when a plump lady with a cheerful face, who had been sitting on the opposite seat, began to speak. 'Your bag has been kept in the top berth. We thought, since it didn't belong to any of us, there would be no harm in placing it on the top berth. I am sorry! Say, your bag was pretty heavy but then I knew right from the beginning that you were a writer. There must be plenty of papers in there.'

Ganga thanked her God and quickly made her way to the top berth. She crouched to hide herself and opened her bag containing her bundle of money. The money was there. Not a paisa had been removed. Ganga climbed down quickly with her bag and sat silently. At the same time, several thoughts started to run at a furious pace in her mind. Seating herself comfortably opposite to the plump woman, Ganga thought to herself – 'How easily my co-passenger has believed that I am a writer! God has been blessed me with an intellectual visage. My odd looking spectacles have definitely saved my day. Simplicity helps. People never delve deep into an issue but always concentrate on the superficial!' The fact was that Ganga did look like an intellectual; sans makeup, less jewellery, wearing large spectacles with her torso wrapped in a simple pink Bengal cotton sari. She was also stunning with curly and dark hair, pouting natural dark pink lips and a face, which shone brighter than the stars.

India in 2007 was still in the grips of a cash based economy. Cash would be held in great esteem till 8 p.m. of Nov 8$^{th}$ of 2016 when demonetisation would strike terror in the lives of hoarders, drug dealers and terrorists and give peace to the honest people. After 2016, India would slowly transition into cash-less economy. But in 2007, Ganga felt profoundly cash rich and happy.

Ganga realized that the world was more concerned about the image portrayed by an individual than the truth about the life of the person.

~ ~ ~

Meanwhile, while Ganga was having all these thoughts, the train had reached Jaipur, the capital of Rajasthan. *Rajasthan was a big land with an area of more than three and a half lakh square kilometers with its ancient Aravallis and the Thar desert.*

Rajasthan with its vibrant colours, set into vibration, Ganga's myriad moods. Soon, Ganga was humming Bollywood tunes and began to feel at home. Afterall, her home in Delhi was still easily accessible. As Ganga walked into an old part of Jaipur town, she saw that the native people were colourfully dressed up. With time, Ganga would realise that this was how the native Rajasthani people were always decked up in these colourful attires and celebrations occurred all the time in the state. Ganga smiled at the belle Rajasthani women - all decked up in the auspicious red colour as well as blue and green colours with plenty of silver on their nose, ears, neck, hands, feet, waist and forehead. To Ganga, every Rajasthani woman began to convey the quintessential Indian lady's love for fancy clothes, jewellery and beauty.

Ganga soon checked into a three star hotel and soon made herself comfortable. It was quite late. So, Ganga went to the dinner buffet, which had been arranged for the guests. Even while the guests were having their dinner, they were entertained by a troupe of traditional Rajasthani dancers. Being a keen observer, Ganga felt that even the eyes of the dancers seemed to dance. The dance of the dazzlingly decorated women, belonging to all age groups and hailing from diverse family backgrounds revitalized Ganga.

Ganga had spent almost a quarter of her life poring through books on different subjects without knowing the practical aspects of living. She wondered as to why people kept searching for happiness when the permanence of beauty lay so near them. Ganga now knew what it was, to experience happiness directly and in good health. There was no experience like experience. 'How much she would have missed had not chance fortune made her to pick up a fight with her family? What a grand opportunity, fate had given her! A lot of positive outcomes were flowing out of one negative event. 'What is negative and what is positive in life?' reflected Ganga. Ganga, the fiery woman from New Delhi was becoming wiser.

Rajasthan made Ganga to think and to reflect upon the philosophical meaning of life. Rajasthan, the land of chivalrous people and the land of bewitching beauty threw Ganga into a tizzy. It brought forth in Ganga, the most extraordinary feelings of strength, courage, love and beauty. Rajasthan was strange and therefore, intensely beautiful. Soon, its sand dunes, forts, hills and palaces and narrow dusty lanes would take her to the bygone era of kings and queens.

Ganga was now also learning to control her hunger, something that she had never been able to do earlier. Now, Ganga never ate unless she was absolutely and honestly hungry. She began to be more frugal, giving more generously to the poor beggars and mendicants. Ganga's goodness brought peace into her life and her beauty increased manifold times. To Ganga, the whole world seemed to relate itself to her. She was beginning to learn to deal with all of humanity as one fraternity and with equanimity. Ganga continued to be her mother's girl - pure, spotless, gracious and dignified. Rajasthan, the land of unending stretches of golden sand was making as much of a deep impact on young Ganga's mind. Ganga recalled the famous lines composed by the great John Keats in his 'Ode on a Grecian Urn' wherein he had said 'Beauty is truth and truth is beauty, that's all ye know on earth and all ye need to know'. It now became clear to her as to why Rajasthan was the favourite tourist destination for everyone especially foreigners. It seemed incredible to her that the lines of Keats were as significant in her own surroundings, in the land of the sandy dunes, as it had been in the earlier times and in another place, far away from her own.

Rajasthan seemed to be the home of colours and Ganga had several fascinating cerebral experiences. Ganga felt like a child destined to walk on the sands of the distant timelessness of the golden land.

At the dargah of Khwaja Moinuddin Chisti, the great Sufi saint at Ajmer, Ganga looked with astonishment at the people belonging to different faiths paying their respects. From Ajmer, Ganga went to a Jain pilgrim centre. The splendid temple of Lord Mahaveer, the twenty forth theerthankara of Jainism had a serene impact on her. The Jain priest at the temple, taught her about the fundamental principles of Jainism including ahimsa, aparigraha, anekart and the law of Karma. Ganga became hungry for more doses of spiritualism, mysticism and enlightenment.

Rajasthan had had a number of local chiefs and this had ensured a regular stream of wars in the sandy sketches of the sun-mauled land. It was quite incredible to Ganga that the land, which had witnessed so much of war, could harbour such a bewildering array of beauty.

Jaipur was a real feast to the seeking eyes of Ganga with its ancient Amer Fort, Hawa Mahal, Jantar Mantar and the city palace. She dreamt about the erstwhile rulers who had ruled the Jaipur region. She began to contemplate a lot. 'How much character would have been tested to bring forth these astounding human creations such as the palaces, forts, paintings, art, architecture, music, dance and statues in this land?' wondered Ganga.

As Ganga's intuitive and analytical mind realized from logical deduction that war and murder was more common in dreaded deserts than in fertile areas. Hunger and deprivation were what forced people from the mauling Mongols to the marauding Afghans to the latest group of terrorists to take to the path of bloodshed.

The glorious story of Sawai Maharaja Jai Singh who belonged to the Kachhawala clan inspired Ganga. She learnt with astonishment, the contributions of the scholar-architect, Vidyadhar Bhattacharya whose architecture of Jaipur based on the Hindu treatise on architecture, Shilpa Shastra still inspired thousands of modern buildings and homes. The complex astronomical instruments built centuries ago were still in working condition.

~ ~ ~

Ganga had some British blood flowing in her veins and arteries. She was an Anglo-Indian. After all, her great great grandfather had been the British collector of Coimbatore. Ganga knew how loyal her community of Anglo-Indians was to India - displaying sometimes even greater loyalty to India than even the native Indians. For Ganga, home was India, not England or America. Inspite of the bewildering differences in the culture and traditions, beliefs and faiths between the Anglo Indian community and the native Indians, the Anglo Indians had acknowledged India as their home. Her great great grandfather had loved India, the country which had nurtured him. Her great great grandfather had just like the English community before him had come to rule India but had eventually fallen in love with it. Instead of merely collecting taxes, he had built hospitals, developed tea estates and built educational institutions for the British as well as for the native Indians. He was known to have never even in an angry mood to have criticised the natives of Madras Presidency. He had always been appreciative of the native Tamil people of Madras Presidency. This was Madras Presidency and he had fallen in love with the Tamil people and who wouldn't - for they were loyal, honest, hardworking, grateful and helpful people. He was in charge of the Madras Regiment in his cantonment and he loved his men and they worshipped him. He was not the typical English collector but one who genuinely cared for India. He was a man in love with two countries: India and Britain. He was never arrogant or cruel. Instead, he was determined, decisive and focussed and liked the natives who loved him, too.

~ ~ ~

Ganga had always had one recurrent dream throughout her life. She would often dream of gold though she had never been to a real gold mine in her entire life. The gold would be running in veins of white rock. The black rock would be discarded. In her dream, she would be going 7800 feet below into a shaft, where huge white rock would contain veins and veins of gold interspersed with silver, zinc and other metals. In her dream, she saw the huge entrance gate with the English name, 'Dawn, Latch and Sons.' She dreamt of going into the Polar Gold Mine in a huge lift with another 119 people, she being on the first stage of the lift. As the materials went up in the huge lift, she was going down on the other side.

*Gold is a very precious metal. Gold is precious because of the importance people have given to gold. Nothing and no one is important unless people decide to make them so. Suddenly, Ganga felt a shove. She woke up from her day-dreaming. She was beginning to understand herself, better.*

Back at the hotel, she ate a plateful of dal batti churma along with bajra chappatis. As she licked the heavy desi ghee off her fingers, Ganga felt a bit warm and satisfied but she still knew that she had a long way to go. Soon after paying the bill, Ganga did not waste time. She booked the night train to Gurgaon in Haryana

~ ~ ~

Soon, she was on her way to Gurgaon. While waiting for the people, she had to almost squeeze herself among several people to get a small foothold space among them. Some lecherous men kept brushing against her, touching her inappropriately, taking advantage of the crowd in the bus. Ganga had to let out, very quietly, her *pet-weapon* against the troublesome Romeos. A few bites here and there, brought peace. Ganga was angry at the licentiousness of the men but there was little that she could do, for this was a long time before the brutal gang rape of a student of physiotherapy in a moving bus at midnight, in the capital of modern India, when ordinary people came out in support of the rape survivor, held candle-light marches and held demonstrations against the government for insufficient action against the perpetrators of the crime and the people's movement was so effective that the government of the day was forced to pass laws in parliament that made more stringent, the laws against perpetrators of heinous crimes like rape. The old regime was soon shown the door by the people of India, who wanted development. The entire system had been shaken up. An enigmatic and charismatic leader would soon usher in a period of great reforms especially against black money and evil forces!

The bus was slowly coming to a halt at the town bus stop, where hundreds of people were either waiting to catch a bus to another town or were getting down. Some others were simply waiting at the bus stop. As the bus drew to the stop, Ganga tried to see the time on her watch. The shadow of a passing tree fell on Ganga's watch and she could not see the time. A minute later, Ganga noted that the time was around 6.00 clock in the evening.

Ganga was feeling enormously hungry and she hurried to a roadside dhabba or food-shop; famous throughout Punjab and Haryana. She felt slightly intimidated by the presence of the large number of men at the dhabba especially truck-drivers and cleaners. Still, Ganga felt safe with her Benevolence near her and then the pressures of her hunger made her resilient to the outside forces. Ganga could have easily eaten in some five-star hotel but she really wanted to experiment with the traditional Indian Punjabi cuisine with the common people. However, there was always a risk of contracting infection from unhygienic food. Thankfully, this was Haryana and the food was clean and good.

She ordered dal, aloo parathas and rice. She also drank a large glass of lassi. It had been a really tasty meal and the sweet buttermilk was really soothing to her throat and body. She felt a sudden wave of exhilaration and of freedom. She remembered with pleasure that her pesky relatives were not around her. After the meal, Ganga left to wash her hands. Benevolence stood near her bag of money and belongings.

During the time when she was cleansing her hands at the washbasin at a corner of the dhabba, there was something going on near her table. A man was stealing her bag!

When Ganga returned, her bag was not where it should have been. Instead, she found her bag of money in someone else's hands. She was at once, angered and upset. She immediately accused the man of trying to steal her money. Suddenly, from nowhere a mob surrounded the twosome. It is quite surprising how crowds appear at the slightest hint of controversy and trouble in India. People quickly take sides, pass judgments and incinerate the weaker of the two conflicting parties. Vested interests would try to make the best use of the opportunity available to them. Ganga requested the crowd to disburse as she felt that she was capable of handling the situation alone. From the beginning, Ganga had never liked outside interferences. Another customer of the hotel explained the situation to Ganga. He had been seated near her when he had seen another man picking up her bag (he did not know what it contained) and leaving! He had demanded an explanation from the man and when he had not been able to elicit a proper explanation, he had forcefully taken away the bag of money from the other man's hand. The thief had run away and here he was, an innocent man caught by the viciousness of suspicious circumstances. Ganga cooled down and apologized. The man forgave her.

Ganga thanked the Good Samaritan after introducing herself. My name is Jo-Ji Philip,' said the man with a half-smile.

'Thank you very much for your complement. It was only my duty,' said Jo-Ji.'I wonder if all people really discharge their duties properly like you. Your sense of honesty and duty is remarkable, 'said Ganga.

From Jo's manner of speaking, Ganga realized that she was speaking to a Malayali. Malayalis are those whose native state is Kerala. Their language is Malayalam.

'You're a Malayali?' asked Ganga.

'Yes, of course,' replied Jo. 'How did you know?'

'I had a number of Malayali friends in school and having interacted with them for years, I can easily find out as to who a Malayali is,' said Ganga.

'You have excellent powers of observation and retention,' said Jo.

'So, what are you doing here? I mean what do you do?' asked Ganga.

'I work as a call centre employee in a big Business Process Outsourcing Centre here in Gurgaon,' said Jo.

'So, how are you here, in Gurgaon?' asked Ganga.

'Oh! My parents and my younger siblings are all in Otttapalam in Kerala. My sisters and brothers are studying and I have to fund their education. I could not find a good job in Kerala for my skills. I had the option of going out to the Middle East but then, I got this job offer and so, I came here to Gurgaon to earn a livelihood. I could have easily found a low paying job, either in my home state or in a nearby state but owing to family pressures, I have to work here in Gurgaon. I feel lonely and depressed. I hate looking at the computer screen for hours and hours. I hate talking to angry customers and to those with all kinds of silly doubts. Sometimes, I feel like I am walking in a tunnel with no end,' said Jo.

'Then, try finding a job for yourself that you want to be doing. Don't do something because society tells you to do that or your family wants you to,' said Ganga. She continued to speak longer. 'Just imagine! Had your siblings been in your position, do you think that they would be willing to sacrifice similarly? I mean staying so far away from family and all that?' asked Ganga.

'I don't know. That's fate,' said Jo.

'So, you believe in destiny and therefore perhaps you do believe in religion, God and so on,' said Ganga.

'Yes, I may a Christian and strongly believe the tenets of my religion but I also do believe, as many Hindus here in India do believe, in the cycle of life and death, rebirth and so on. I believe in Karma, Dharma and Moksha,' said Jo.

Ganga was duly impressed with the secular spirit of the young man and continued. Though she scarcely knew Jo, she felt an immediate bond with Jo.

It was quite late, around midnight when the duo parted. 'What a parting and what a meeting? Truly, the world is full of unexpected situations, people and feelings. No matter, how much one compels destiny to be the servant; it remains our one true master,' thought Ganga. The two youngsters promised to keep in touch with each other.

Ganga and Jo-Ji were two human beings who had been bonded together by the universal feelings of fraternity; the same bond, which unites every soul in this earthy plane.

After a long search, Ganga found a good hotel room to stay. She gave instructions to the receptionist to have her breakfast sent to her room by eight, the next morning. She began to sleep and she began to dream of the rising sun, of quiet dawns and dusks, her new friend, the shadowy twilight, milk sweetmeats made by her mother, her home, her dog, her friends and of what all she could gain: gold, treasure, fortune, fun, friends, diamonds, rubies, emeralds, pearl...beauteous nature....

Ganga woke up in her hotel room in Haryana. She felt refreshed and joyous. She brushed her teeth, took a lovely scented bath and then ordered dal, chapattis, rice and chutney.

Ganga got ready to see the most important places in Gurgaon. It was the most happening place with Business Process outsourcing centres at every corner of the dynamic region. The youngsters who worked in the call centres worked continuously into the night with their customers who stayed thousands of kilometres away from where they were. There was on one hand, exuberance and momentum and on the other, loss of values and loneliness.

After a bit of sight-seeing in Gurgaon, Ganga boarded the train to Panipat.

CHAPTER

*Nineteen*

## More Understanding

At last, the train halted at Panipat. As soon as Ganga seated herself in the tourist bus to go to the exact place of the battlefield, she began to visualize the past of the destination that she was about to reach. She took out her old history text and as she read from the section on Mughal history, she began to feel more excited to be where she was. 'In 1526 A.D., Zahir-ud-din Babur had defeated Ibrahim Lodi and had established the supreme Mughal Empire, which ruled successfully for several centuries. Again in 1556, Babur's grandson did it again by defeating Hemu, whose army had thought that their king was dead when they saw the caparisoned elephant of the king without its highly esteemed passenger. During the third battle of Panipat, the powerful Ahmad Shah Abdali had trounced the Marathas, the nationalists on their own turf. The soil is always faithful to the chivalrous and has no strength of its own. It derives its strength from those who rule her.' Ganga imagined the great emperors dressed up in silken robes and adorned with heavy pearls - that all wars are futile, in the end.

~ ~ ~

The month was September and the sky was dull. The weather was beginning to become colder. Ganga continued reading. 'Kurukshetra was yet another battlefield where the legendary Pandavas had defeated their deceiving cousins -one hundred Kaurava brothers!'

Ganga seemed to understand the reasons for India's expanding population. Having many children was part of the Indian psyche. Children were considered a source of security and a source of happiness for their parents. Ganga however knew that the teeming population was also a cause of poverty of the millions.

After, a few days in Haryana, Ganga left for Punjab – the land of five rivers.

~ ~ ~

Punjab with its fertile golden fields, myriad flowers and beautiful people women welcomed Ganga. The prosperity in the land of lassi, roti and ghee warmed the heart of Ganga. Ganga was turning to be a connoisseur of all the good things in life. Punjab of the Indian land was the land of five rivers including the legendary and most famous 'Indus' river. In fact, 'India' itself, had its name derived from the name of the river.

Ganga's first stop was the Golden Temple at Amritsar. The overwhelming prosperity of Punjab set Ganga's spirit into a jubilant mood. Ganga ate her meals at the public food-house or the 'langar', a custom started by the Sikh Gurus. She was quite taken aback at the endless supply of food from the langar to all men, women and children of all regions, religions and races who had come to the temple. It was then that Ganga realized that the silly barriers of religious pride break down in the cauldron of humanity.

It was the Sikh religious Guru Ram Das, who had established Amritsar. The mere sight of the Golden Temple helps to salvage some of the lost sensibilities and sensitivities of the soul-sick.

There were many gorgeous places in Punjab, a place that seemed to have been overwhelmingly blessed with the gifts of nature. The golden fields of wheat would be sufficient to supply the entire wheat needs of India. All the Punjabis, as Ganga noted, were incredibly strong and Ganga attributed their strength to wheat.

~ ~ ~

From Punjab, Ganga's next destination was Jammu and Kashmir. Jammu and Kashmir, the most integral part of India was actually a combination of three composite zones, Jammu, Kashmir and Ladakh. Jammu had always been the state's winter capital and Srinagar, the summer capital. Ladakh with its monks and mind-blowing monasteries was a world in itself.

Ganga had read a lot about Jammu and Kashmir in the two most perfect books about Kashmir: Rajatarangini by Kalhana and Nilmat Purana. The history of Kashmir could be ascertained from the two books alone. The outstanding king of Kashmir,

Lalithaditya had constructed beautiful structures and had improvised and had brought in new systems of irrigation. Zain-ud-Abedin was the most famous Muslim ruler of Kashmir.

Beauty lies in the eyes of the beholder and beauty dazzles where virtue predominates. The countryside of Kashmir was a showstopper. It was such a beautiful sight and Ganga's searching eyes devoured the beauty of the villages. The magnificence of what she saw seeped into her body and soul through her eyes. It was surprising but she realised to her profound bewilderment that she had been yearning, all her life to be in such a place, experiencing such sublime beauty. The strange tranquillity of the place was joyously fulfilling. The whole countryside was blissfully sleepy and Ganga liked this aspect the most. She thought it would be a beautiful idea to live in Kashmir in her final days; amongst the wild grass, trees, flowers, birds and children.

The beauty of Kashmir assuaged her ruffled sentiments. The pristine silvery waters of the glaciers, the synchronized singing of the lonely birds, the pure air, the pines and firs on the floppy-sloppy mountain tracks, the tired tourists, the tracks of snow leopards and the sight of the Himalayas.

Ganga waited for the winter to intensify and then she left with thousands of fellow pilgrims to Amarnath. Ganga saw the famed icy lingams, one of the enduring forms of Lord Shiva; famed and worshipped throughout India. Kashmir was truly the paradise on earth.

# CHAPTER

## *Twenty*

## *The Heart of India*

Uttar Pradesh is a place with the history of India in its arteries. Uttar Pradesh is full of temples, pilgrim centers, sanctuaries, parks, dirt, dust, pollution, population, overcrowding and all. Uttar Pradesh is home to the famous Golden Kashi Vishwanath temple dedicated to Lord Shiva, in the form of Shivling. This temple was destroyed several times in the past by the Muslim rulers and was rebuilt in 1776 by Rani Ahalya Bai Holkar. There is even a shrine dedicated to the Goddess Annapurna or the Mother of food and all things good. It is not without reason that Uttar Pradesh is as blessed as it is cursed. Everything lies in the hands of the people. This is the heart of India, the birth place of India's first Prime Minister, Jawaharlal Nehru, a land more ancient and timeless than time, itself. It was here that great seers had done their tapas and brought the gods to visit them on the earth.

It was in the wee hours of a cold winter morning that Ganga reached Ayodhya, the birthplace of Lord

Ram, the God of millions of Hindus. It was there that she met her Guru, Shri Ramananda Swami who would go on to teach her Indian astrology.

As Ganga walked on the streets of Ayodhya, she marvelled at the sense of timeless spirituality, which had encapsulated the ancient town. He was sitting peacefully chanting some Hindu mantras holding a rosary in his hand. She felt a strange power pull her towards him.

Ganga quickly befriended him. He taught her the basic tenets of Indian astrology. Surprisingly, her Guruji was also an expert in palmistry. He began with his lesson on the nine planets. Guruji handed over to her, a small book. 'Let me give you the horoscope of Lord Rama, the king of all Ayodhya. Tell me as to what you understand from the Rasi chart.' said Swami ji in a mild voice. The piece of paper contained a box diagram and a few words were written on them. It all seemed like Greek and Latin to Ganga and of course, there was no prior chance of her knowing much about astrology. In fact, Ganga was not at all superstitious and had never believed in accepting fate or astrology or anything of that sort. To her, astrology and horoscope reading were merely ways of deceiving the human psyche and filling it with unknown fears or new expectations. After learning a few concepts in astrology from Guruji, Ganga began to believe in the impact of planets on human lives. Ganga held out her hand and asked, 'Guruji, I have heard that you can read the lines in a palm, 'Tell me, what is in my fate?'

Guruji replied, 'Your line of destiny goes straight from the wrist. It is well marked, indicating luck, brilliance, success and all that you desire, my child.'

Ganga asked Guruji, 'Do you really mean what you say?'

Guruji replied, 'I am not a soothsayer but I know the art of reading palms well and the lines of destiny never lie.'

Now, Ganga became very interested in Indian astrology. Maybe it was because, now she had a reason to want to learn it. *She had always, always craved for adoration and the like and if astrology would help her to gain greater self-belief, then why not know more about it?* Maybe, she would be able to help others, too to gain greater confidence and clarity about their respective futures.

'Guruji, tell me more about this. Vedic astrology and all,' continued Ganga.

Guruji began to speak in a solemn and deep voice but just audible to his new disciple.

'Listen, my child. Listen. Vedic astrology is an ancient science. It is not a perfect science but nevertheless, it is a science. It is experimental and inferences can be drawn. You can take anyone's natal horoscope and be able to read their future but maybe not perfectly. A correct understanding of the placement of the planets can give us a reasonably clear idea, where the native is headed in life. Knowing astrology is like travelling on a known ocean but one just cannot say what exactly will happen on the journey but there will be many pointers. That's what astrology is. It is a pointer to the many things a native is destined for. For instance, if a person has Amsavatara yoga, then such a person is destined for greatness - he or she is like a partial avatara or incarnation. But they are just ordinary people. They are not avataras of the stature of Rama, the prince-turned king of Ayodhya or like Krishna of Dwaraka. We all know of the various incarnations of the Hindu God, Vishnu. Rama, Krishna and Parasurama are all incarnations of the protector, Vishnu. In matsya avatara, Vishnu took the form of a fish and in Koorma avatara, he took the form of a boar. Vishnu even took the fearsome form of half lion-half man known as Narasimha Avatara. The tenth avatara who is awaited is Kalki. Even the Buddha is considered by many Hindus as an avatara of Vishnu but that is false and wrong. An attempt is being made to subsume Buddhism into Hinduism. But Hinduism and Buddhism are two very different religions. In Hinduism, the emphasis is on ritualism. In Buddhism, the emphasis is on truth and goodness. Also in Buddhism, there is no concept of soul whereas Hindus believe in rebirth using the soul concept. In Hinduism, the emphasis is on spiritualism and materialism whereas in Buddhism, emphasis is on the spiritual alone. Given a choice, I would have been happier if I was born a Buddhist rather than a Hindu,' said the Guru with a twinkle in his eyes. 'All these incarnations of Vishnu were taken in order to establish goodness and to destroy the evil forces. God keeps coming to earth in different forms to protect the goodness and to destroy evil. However, those with 'amsavatara yoga' are special people - partial incarnations of the God - men and women, born to help the good and to punish the people. Funnily, they are very passionate people but they know how to keep their passions under control. They are sociable people but being intelligent and knowing the vagaries of human behaviour know whom to trust and how much to trust. They are die-hard romantics, kind and gentle but they know how to control their emotions. They are philosophical people and ask profound questions about life, its purpose, dharma, svadharma, adharma, death and even after-life,' revealed Guruji.

Ganga was extremely elated to learn about this astrological yoga and she, like most of us are, became intensely curious to know if she too, had amsavatara yoga.

'Guruji, do you think I have this yoga? Do tell me about other yogas, planets, the impact of planets in various houses and everything you know. I am hugely, interested.'

Guruji replied, 'It all depends on your natal chart. The timing of what will happen depends on the dashas or the long periods of the influence of a particular planet. But the area where a lot of people go wrong is the careless way of noting down of the birth time of a child. Unless, the correct birth place and time, an astrologer cannot make the right predictions. Vedic astrology has been given by great sages of India, who knew more about astronomy than modern space scientists. Varahamihira and Parashara were some of the great astrologer-saints of ancient India. India as we all know is one of the most ancient cultures of the world and has contributed more to world peace and harmony than any country in the world. While war was propagated in most parts of the world, to establish orderliness, India used peace. The two greatest ambassadors of peace that the world has ever known, Gandhiji and The Buddha were both born in India. The peace that India has contributed to the world is immeasurable. The so-called economically developed nations with vast military prowess and capabilities are nothing compared to India. They may have made more material progress but India is the spiritual guide for the world'.

A lot of wrong predictions are made because of bad astrologers, who know little and pretend to know more and because of the callous attitude of family members, who don't note down the birth time of a child properly. It may also because that a large number of people still don't know to see the time. Now coming to the case of the amsavatara yoga, you need to have Venus and Jupiter in angular positions to the ascendant also known as the lagan, in Vedic astrology. Also, the planet of justice, Saturn must be in a Kendra and that too, exalted, leading to yoga know as sasa yoga. So, anyone who has amsavatara yoga has to necessarily have sasa yoga, too. In addition to the above two conditions, a third condition must be fulfilled and that is to have your lagna in a chara sign or movable signs. There are just four chara signs; aries or mesha, cancer or kataka, libra or thula and capricorn or makara. Give me a copy of your horoscope if you have one with you. Otherwise, give me the details such as latitude and longitude of your birth place and your birth time and I will have your horoscope cast in no time.'

Of course, Ganga had no copy of her natal horoscope. She had not expected all this to happen. She had not known that she would meet such a sincere Guru, in these modern times. Nevertheless, there were certain things that Ganga knew about Vedic Astrology. Her mother had taught her a few basics. Her great grandfather had been a famous astrologer.

Ganga hailed from a quite orthodox Brahmin family, which amalgamated well with some already existing English genes. The Panchang or the Almanac was the second most widely read book in her house, next to the Bhagwad Gita, one of the world's great religious books. She knew about Jupiter, the planet who gave luck. Jupiter is the biggest planet in the solar system. It was the well-known planet for wealth, health, success and family. So, literally, this was the top guy, who would go about benevolently helping people. She knew about Saturn, having seen more cruel and evil people going around, doing pooja to please the Lord Saturn, who was the punisher of the unjust and the upholder of justice. In one of the Indian states, Ganga had observed a large number of temples for Saturn. It gave her an idea about the kind of people, who lived there.

Ganga said, 'Do you think, Guruji, that these planets can help free us from our sins?'

Guruji said, 'No, never. Planets and Gods help the righteous and to help those, who are confused and don't know the path of virtue. No one can save those, who commit sin on purpose - who are incorrigible. There is no religion in this world, which says that God will protect the sinners if they will surrender to him. No one and nothing can save us from our sins and that is the reality of life. We keep going on this journey called life without knowing what is going to happen. We have only hope and courage to guide us. Undoubtedly, hope and courage are the two things, which can protect us.'

Ganga spoke.' Guruji, I have met a lot of evil people in life; liars, sinners, selfish people, cruel men, arrogant, unhelpful people in life. I have seen several sinners praying fervently to the Gods, doing pooja for hours and not feeding one hungry child or throwing stones at poor animals! Enough of this dichotomy!'

'Cruelty cannot be explained easily and let me tell you one thing. Sinners can never be spiritual. They will never attain deliverance and they will keep suffering in many ways over many births,' said Guru ji.

Over the next few days, Ganga learnt many things from Guru ji! The next day, she returned to meet Guru Ramji. She had just reread a little book of astrology, which she had purchased in one of the many, small bylanes of Ayodhya.

She learnt more about Rahu, the snake headed north node demon with a human body. She also learnt about the human headed south node demon with the snake body, Ketu. Rahu was the creator of illusions. He was the one, who led people to try out the bad things such as narcotics, smoking and drinking. He was the bad guy; the vilest in the group. Compared to Rahu, Saturn was an angel, who merely punished the evil and rewarded the good. Saturn was the strict teacher - kind and benevolent to the good and obedient children and harsh with the bad kids. Ganga now learnt about Mars, the planet of courage and other planets.

The next day, Guruji was glad to see her again. After enquiring if she had had her breakfast, he started speaking.

'Today, I will teach you about a great yoga but it is not pertaining to the planets.' He smiled at Ganga's look of confusion. He then continued. 'The explanation for this is in the Bhagvad Gita. A karma yogi is one, who lives in the material world but remains detached. It does really matter whether you are in a state of renunciation or amidst wordly pleasures. What really matters is whether your heart is pure. A pure heart can defeat a thousand evils. It is only important that a person remains anchored in the fundamentals of truth and justice and the whole world listens to such a person. This is the message that Lord Krishna gave to Arjuna, the great warrior-archer. The true yogi is one, who is free from depression. A yogi has to purposefully connect himself to happiness. The real purpose of yoga is to make steady, the unsteady mind and keep it happy. Even the ordinary householder can attain moksha by merely following his svadharma and dharma. Don't depend on the planets. Depend on yourself.'

'What is the difference between svadharma and dharma? asked Ganga.

'Svadharma is that action, which is in accordance with your nature. Dharma refers to righteousness or those duties, which a particular person is expected to do; for instance, the duties of a son or father etcetera. You must read our ancient scriptures, the Vedas and their commentaries, the Upanishads,' replied Guruji.

Ganga asked Guruji about happiness. He replied that happiness was not just a destination but its own path. 'Happiness' is how you approach life. It is not just in materialist pleasures. In this, I differ from many sages, who say that material things don't give pleasures. Of course, they do but money alone can never give happiness. Money and love; both together make a person happy. The love that I am referring to does not mean pleasing anyone but what you do for a person to increase their welfare. True love is giving without expectation.'

'How can giving without any quid-pro-quo make us happy?' asked Ganga.

'One day, you shall experience,' said Guruji. 'The mastery of the mind is possible only through love,' said Guruji and abruptly ended the conversation.

Soon, Ganga set off for Ghaziabad in Uttar Pradesh, the heart of India. Ghaziabad was a bustling city with its busy roads and management students. There were several training institutes in the city. Ganga stayed for a night in one of the hotels there. The food was not too good and she felt uneasy. Probably, there had been some food contamination and Ganga had affected by food poisoning. The resident doctor in the hotel cured her ailment almost immediately with some herbal juice but Ganga was so scared that she decided to escape from the place as soon as possible. Ghaziabad with its teeming population and unclean eateries did not feel like heaven for Ganga. *Gruesome are the effects of over population and overcrowding.*

~ ~ ~

Agra, the land of the Taj Mahal had always been so near and yet so out of reach for Ganga. Her busy working parents had never been able to take out a few minutes out of their busy schedules for their only daughter. It was not as if Ganga was blaming her parents but things were just the way they were. Today, the Taj beckoned her and she would not miss the opportunity. It was a majestic and alluring structure but it was no preparation for the most wondrous sight that Ganga was to witness: The 'Fatehpur Sikri' or the 'City of Victory'.

Fatehpur Sikri was near Agra. The great emperor, Akbar who was a man of several worthy accomplishments, had built the city of Victory. Akbar was not literate but he was more educated than several of the most learned and knowledgeable men of his era. Akbar, the great had learnt a lot from his conversations with the intellectually accomplished men of his kingdom. Fatehpur Sikri seemed to Ganga, the perfect place for a monarch of the status of Emperor Akbar to be. It had the Diwan-i-am and the Diwan-i-khas. The Emperor, Akbar had held his court in the Diwan-i-am. Ganga learnt this from her guide, Abdullah, who told her that the acoustics of the place was so good that the king sitting on the throne could hear every word spoken by the members of the public audience, which sat even a kilometre away from the king. Emperor Akbar had married Hindus, Muslims, Christians and even a Turkish woman. On all the walls, there were several hundred designs of earrings and necklaces and Ganga watched several modern age jewellery-designers at work sitting in the heat and the cold just to copy the designs and to use them in their own masterpieces. Ganga tried to imagine what Emperor Akbar's harem would have looked like but for some reason could not successfully conjure up the images.

Ganga also availed of the opportunity to visit Mathura, the birthplace of Lord Krishna. Krishna was a celebrated Indian Hindu God whose life was celebrated by millions, world over. Of course, Ganga's joy had been even more manifold when she had stepped into the city of Ayodhya, which was the birthplace of the legendary noble King, Lord Rama, the king of all of Ayodhya. Lord Rama was the epitome of virtuousness and his level of chastity and love for Sita was eulogized the world over. The eternal and faithful love of Rama towards Sita, his wife and the faithfulness of the chaste wife towards her husband was what made the billions of people, the world over worship them. Till date, Lord Rama was the most worshipped God of the Hindus in India.

At Allahabad, Ganga, once again took a dip in the holy Ganges at the confluence of three rivers- Ganga, Yamuna and the mythical Saraswati. She was astonished to see a large number of sages and learned scholars who were able to live with cancerous cells on their head or on their necks. The tumours were visible and protruding outside. These people as Ganga found out were able to resist their dangerous disease without going in for any kind of medical treatment. Ganga realized that will power was more essential in fighting diseases than anything else. *Faith would definitely cure.*

Ganga could easily identify the different colours of the rivers when they mingled at Sangam. Ganga was bluish-white in colour, very pure. Yamuna, as a result of the years of industrial effluents flowing into it was almost pitch-black in colour.

# CHAPTER

## *Twenty One*

### Going Deep into History

As she travelled, Ganga read more and more books her motherland, its history, its geography, its culture and all. She was especially fascinated by the Indian history. Until the day, Ganga had left Delhi on her seemingly absurd mission, Ganga had been a really ordinary girl with ordinary desires, ordinary feelings, ordinary perceptions, and ordinary inclinations, who had been in a perpetual state of mundane existence. She had not known the vastness of life and its tremendous diversity until the current frame of time. Now, she knew that the world was wide with billions and billions of perspectives. It was only now after Ganga had left the comfort of her home that she realized the need to take care of herself, to understand problems from other people's points of view and to equip herself with the most potent weapon in the whole universe, which is knowledge arising out of moral strength. To keep herself engaged during her travels, Ganga was reading more books, now than she had ever before. By now, Ganga had finished reading the 'The Da Vinci Code' by Dan Brown and Cheiro's 'Palmistry'. Ganga's knowledge of mysticism was growing and she was now an expert in palmistry, vaastu, numerology and astrology in addition to her poetic skills. Ganga was now a devotee of this new and wholesome science of the stars. She started to believe that it was through the planets of the solar system that God controlled the fate of the earthlings. Astrology, be it Vedic or Chinese or Western, it was like an ocean: endless and infinite in scope.

History was very fascinating for variegated reasons for Ganga. *'One, for the fact that history has a knack of repeating itself at irregular intervals.'*

Second, Ganga recognized the fact that great people who were able to accomplish much during their lives were the ones who had studied the trends in history and who knew that learning from experience was the best way of learning and that one would have to learn from one's mistakes and to correct oneself. One should not repeat mistakes. Ganga learnt that India was not just urbane with its pomp, glory and money but was also rural where the majority of the people lived, worked and earned. The velocity of circulation of money was biased in favour of the city with its furniture marts, fruits and vegetables; markets, shopping malls, cinema theatres, shops, factories, companies and industries. The villages did not possess the power to cope with the pecuniary prowess of the cities. Ganga, an ardent devotee of the policies of the Scientist-President of India, Dr.A.P.J.Abdul Kalam believed that the provision of urban facilities like education, health, water and sanitation in the rural areas would be the ideal way to assuage the tired and hurt feelings of the rural dwellers of India. Ganga understood that India would soon become a great superpower once it would gain the expertise of bringing about a hand-in-glove relationship between the urban moods with its richness and rural traditions with its sense of morals and agricultural prosperity.

'Modern India had witnessed many struggles. There were many problems, which were being faced by the Indians during their search for the elusive freedom. The problems had been of different types: social, economic, political, psychological and religious. Sociologically, India was a country divided on the basis of caste and religion, the latter being the legacy of the white conquerors. The Indian nationalistic sentiments finally evolved themselves into a group, which was named as the Indian National Congress. By then, there was a sincere and comprehensive desire on the behalf of the Indians for political, social and economic progress. In fact, the very same kind of feelings permeated the Indian spirits before independence kindling the spirit of Indians and setting their blood on boil. The non-cooperative attitude of the imperial rulers had stunned the core of the Indian psyche. All kind of brutalities had been borne silently and the Indians waited silently for an opportunity to make a comeback to make the British go back. The Indians harnessed all their skills, which manifested in a large number of forms such as the non-cooperative movement, the civil disobedience and the Quit India Movement where the motto was either to free India or to die in the attempt. It was the contribution of leaders like the non-violent Gandhiji and the human mountain of courage, Subhash Chandra Bose that saw India getting freedom for he dared to pay back on the same coin to his opponents. The slender backs of India's multitudinous farmers had been exposed to the heat of the heavy land revenue policies of the British. Brilliant leaders like Ban Gangadhar Tilak, Rabindranath Tagore and Swami Vivekananda had blazed their way through the brutal bullying of the masters creating a new space for themselves seeking deliverance for the hapless Indians. Slavery was a thing of the past, to be remembered in the subconscious and for consciousness to be free and fair. Imperialism was now nothing but a relic.'

The 1905 Partition of Bengal snowballed into an unending flurry of anxious moments in Indian nationalism. Terrorism took the form of assassinations and bombings. The hands of the malignant and monstrous minds, which desired to curb every freedom loving instinct of the Indians, hanged militants like Asafulla Khan, Ramprasad Bismil, Roshan Singh and Rajendra Singh who were involved in the Kakori conspiracy case. The Assistant Superintendent of

Police, Saunders who had been considered as the perpetrator of the most heinous of all crimes, on Lala Lajpat Rai was murdered by the lovers of freedom. Raj Guru and Bhagat Singh, the masterminds behind the attacks along with Sukhdev were executed. Terrorist movements abroad had gathered momentum.

The reforms of 1901 did not actually benefit the Indians and did not provide for any kind of official majority in the councils. It was mere eyewash. In 1906, with the formation of the Indian Muslim League, communalism assumed ugly dimensions. In 1916, the Congress joined the Muslim League and the moderates and the extremists came together.

Social reformers like Raja Ram Mohan Roy, Debendranath Tagore, Keshab Chandra Sen, Henry Vivian Derozio and Iswar Chandra Vidyasagar had brought with them, new ways of thinking, the opposition to the caste system, the opposition to the system of child marriage, the support to widow remarriages, girl's education and the destruction of the Sati system and anti-polygamy. Indian nationalism had gathered tremendous strength as a result of the tussle between the old and the new ways of thinking.

Mahatma Gandhi with his Satyagraha had revolutionized the Indian freedom struggle and had made an unmistakably perfect impression on the Indian psyche. Non-violence and truth, the same truths that had guided the Buddha and the Mahavira, the principles practised by the great Mahatma had an entire nation lying prostrate before this seemingly feeble man; not out of fear but out of respect for the man, whose greatest weapon was moral force. The violence of Chauri-chaura had made the Mahatma to withdraw his body of faithful followers from the non-cooperation movement and the Civil disobedience movement of the Mahatma galvanized India and drew a tremendous response from the Indians.'

These untiring and restless thoughts slowly tired out Ganga's mind and body and soon they treated themselves to the most beautiful of human comforts; sleep.

CHAPTER

# *Twenty Two*

## *The Ancient Treasure House*

Bihar was Ganga's next stop after Uttar Pradesh. With every destination and the mind's milestone associated with it, Ganga found herself becoming more and more confident about her own self. Ganga's fears in some cases, as she was able to find out, during the course of her travels, were well founded and in many others, they were being proved wrong. Bihar, one of the oldest and most sacred places on the earth was going to be a real eye opener for Ganga. Bihar had been one of the most prosperous states in erstwhile India and there was in fact, a view among the great political analysts in those days, which were confirmed by the happenings of the day that anyone who could rule over Magadha would be able to exercise control over the whole of India. Bihar had been the epitome of prosperity. Alas! What Ganga saw in Bihar could no longer bring any sweet reminiscences of the state's past for she saw great poverty. The bigger Bihar had been badly mauled and made into a smaller one.

Ganga got down in Patna. The Patna railway station was overcrowded with the milling crowds, porters and railway staff. There was a lot of trade unionism in Patna. She checked herself into a small hotel on a busy street. A prominent State Party's headquarters was located in the street. There were prominent banners and posters everywhere. There appeared to be some paid goons, who seemed to be going in wandering in the area. A clash was imminent. Ganga knew that all places in India were not safe. She took the wise decision of moving out of the place. Over the next couple of days, Ganga went out shopping, visited temples and visited tourist spots. Out of whatever interaction that she had with the Bihari people be it the vendors, the guides, the shop keepers or the people on the street, she found in the people of Bihar, a strange and child-like goodness and innocence in its people. Ganga savoured their goodness with a spirit full of respect.

Ganga followed the footsteps of the Buddha as she traced his steps from Bodh Gaya to Gaya to Kusinagara. Ganga thanked the Lord Buddha for all his compassion and for leading her in the right path; the Ashtamarga or the Eight fold path. At Gaya, Ganga watched the Hindus offer oblation for the salvation of their dead ancestors.

Ganga travelled as far as the Indo-Nepalese border and though she herself did not go into Nepal crossing the border, she learnt that there were many number of people making the trip to either of the two sides. Ganga also visited the battlefield of Buxar, where the great battle of Buxar had taken place with a significant impact of enormous magnitude on the lives of the over-flowing-with-passion Indians. Ganga made the mandatory trip to Rajgir and Nalanda and tried imagining how quiet and perfect the place would have been with its scholars in the universities in the bygone years. There were fewer people in the past. Population had only recently increased in such a geometric population. There would have been no traffic congestion or pollution. Hiueng Tsang, the great Chinese traveler had studied in the Nalanda University. Ganga's heart and mind desired to stay in the serene place for long years with the same aim of the great scholars, who had once honoured the place with their presence and tremendous spirit. At Vikramashila, Ganga saw the ruins of the ancient university of higher learning. At Sasaram, she saw the tomb of Sher Shah Suri, the king who had been able to resist and win some important battles against the great Mughal Emperor, Humayun himself. Sher Shah Suri had been a man of immense accomplishments and he had always been a friend of the travelers. Finally, Ganga returned to see Patna in all its prowess; the modern version of the ancient Pataliputra where the king, Chandragupta Maurya had lived and reigned from his golden palace, whereas his Guru and kingmaker – the most machiavellian man, Kautilya stayed in a hut to bridge the gap between the hut and palace and to hold high, the mighty Maurya empire. After travelling for a while, Ganga finally decided that she should stay in one place for some time.

Like a nomad, Ganga kept travelling. Soon, Ganga made Calcutta, her base. To her, Calcutta was the gateway to the northeast. Ganga realized that Calcutta was astounding and it was invoking in her, several thousand kinds of emotions responses from her. She knew that she wouldn't be able to judge the city in a few hours or days and that she would need more time to understand its repertoire of talents, people and emotional messages. Ganga would return to Kolkata after some time.

Ganga had heard little about the northeast. She looked at the Indian map and noticed that the northeast was not exactly very near. In fact, one would have to go around Bangladesh's northern boundary, in order to reach the northeast. Ganga made a mental outline of where would go first. 'Yes, this would be right place to begin exploring the most unexplored part of my country'. She knew that she would not be able to travel all over the north-east. She thought that she could at least visit a few areas of the north east like the beautiful state of Assam!

Ganga's first halt was Gangtok, the capital of Sikkim. Sikkim was very beautiful. Seeing the glorious Khargchendzonga mountain in the Singalila Range was a heart-stopping moment for Preetha. As the tourist bus drew near the much-worshipped mountain range, a kind of awe fell over the tourists. Ganga had expected that the sense of awe would get evoked for she knew that it was in human nature to feel overawed by something supreme, tremendous and venerable. The snowy peak of the glorious Khangchendzonga seemed to touch the sky and the heavens seemed to lean over desperately in a bid to embrace its towering child. Ganga ate ice cream in the blistering cold and thoroughly enjoyed the delightful experience. It seemed to Ganga, a cool idea to eat ice cream and watch the beauty of the snowy, lustrous mountain. Suddenly, something flew before Ganga's eyes. She thought it was her imagination that was playing tricks on her and that she had finally succumbed to her exhaustion. It wasn't the case. It was a blue verditer flycatcher; a lovely blue bird with a pretty beak.

The pristine peaks, the voluptuous valleys, the lazy lakes and the rapacious rivers lightened the burdened human hearts. Ganga was able to visit Sikkim's most venerated shrine: The Tastiding Monastery. Usually, there were also a number of festivals that were continuously going on in Sikkim. However since it was the month of December, Ganga could see only the Long festival. If she had been able to visit Sikkim in October or November, she would have seen two more festivals, Duchen and Teoha. Since she did not know about them, she did not miss them. In life, we often don't miss what we don't know.

One of the strange things that Ganga noticed in Sikkim was that all the monasteries had their walls filled with paintings. These paintings, as Ganga noticed, seemed out of the world and those included paintings of horse-headed men with musical stringed instruments. The paintings were all very vivid and seemed to convey more than one meaning. The paintings were all unsigned. The evil characters in the paintings had drawn out swords and conspicuously large teeth. It was all so weird and compellingly frightening. What Ganga did not know was that the art of the northeast and countries like Bhutan was never about bringing recognition to the artist. Later, Ganga went to see the Rumtek Monastery and was enraptured at the colours and contours of the peace-invoking structures.

~ ~ ~

Soon, Ganga was on her way to Assam. Ganga had now changed a bit from the kind of girl that she used to be. Her vivaciousness was of a more mellowed nature. She was seeing more and more of the real world by now. It was a bus journey that she had opted for and that was because Ganga wanted to see all the places all along the route and so she did. The bus meandered through Jaldhapar, Koch Bihar, Manas, Bongaigaon, Guwahati and finally the bus reached Dispur. En route, she saw the great river, Brahmaputra and noticed how powerful, it was. Its torso seemed to have become resilient to the pressures of human existence and unlike most rivers; it didn't seem to like the idea of compromise on any of its virtues. The majestic river also commanded immense respect from the people who never dared to trespass its vast properties. Brahmaputra was thus, a huge vibrant giant who never hurt the people unless they dared to play tricks with it. The Brahmaputra, literally translated as the 'son of the Brahma or the son of the creator', was really a jewel of a creation with its enormity spread over several countries. The Brahmaputra was the lifeline of Bangladesh, India as well as Tibet. To Ganga, just as the river Ganga was the epitome of gentleness, the river, Brahmaputra was the epitome of endless power, strength and beauty. Yet the Brahmaputra had never attained the kind of fame that the river, Ganges had the fortune of receiving. Looking out of her window in the dusty bus, Ganga felt like an atom in front of a colossus. 'Who would not be carried away the ravishing wonder that is the Brahmaputra?' She took out her pen from her handbag and a beautiful poem on the great river began to flow out of her pen and at a breathless pace.

**'*The Brahmaputra*'**

Life is Brahmaputra!

Wide, large, infinite;

Perilous beauty!

That is the Brahmaputra,

The Brahmaputra is YOU!


The Brahmaputra is an emporium,

Of the trials and triumphs of humanity,

Encased in timelessness,

Giving its gifts for free!

The Brahmaputra is the vivid imagination,

Of childhood years,
Its fructification,
In the maturing years!

Magnificent like persons of great eminence,
The Brahmaputra is a revelation.

The Brahmaputra is a permanent image,
In the annals of enamelled time,
It is a light,
It is a song.

The Brahmaputra is a million-limbed vision,
Of multitudinous magnificence,
Like the million-petalled Sun-God
A guidance to tranquillity!

The Brahmaputra is the penetrating heavens,
Moving in and out of the human experience,
The proof of the living conscience.

The Brahmaputra is beauty,
Dipped deep in divinity,
The Mother of emotions,
The Father of thought.

The Brahmaputra is the Frail Human-being,
With all her shortcomings,
Dance of fantasy and reality,
Drowned in the dainty dance of eternity.

The Brahmaputra is birth and death,
It is the beginning and the end,
The end of the beginning and
The beginning of the end.

The Brahmaputra is Lord Ganesha,
The highest wisdom of humanity.
The Brahmaputra is the waterfall of beauty,
The grand heights of human sublimity.

The Brahmaputra is the ocean of infinite joy,
Immeasurable, full of lasting love.

The Brahmaputra is Truth,
The highest Truth conceivable in human vision.

The Brahmaputra is the Light from the Heavens,
Descended on the earth,
To free the ailing and the suffering,
From their wretchedness.

The Brahmaputra is the distilled wisdom of the sages,
From the ages.

The Brahmaputra is the shadows shattered,
Brought into reality.

The Brahmaputra is the unfailing lamp,
Guiding us to our destinations,
Through the path of tribulations,
Leading to Final and Total Triumph.

The Brahmaputra is the creator of all human
experiences,
Merging and submerging,
The Brahmaputra is Brahman, Himself.

The Brahmaputra is the story of India,
The epic story of Ramayana,
It is the blend of antiquity,
And modernity.

The Brahmaputra is an aspiration,
A Bodhisattva,
The dance of Lord Shiva,
Dissolving dark dimensions.

The Brahmaputra is a happy child,
Playing in the lap of Mother Nature,
The Brahmaputra is our Mother,
Who gives us warmth, food and shelter.

The Brahmaputra is the song divine,
Dissolving space and time.

The Brahmaputra is the culmination of all human aspirations,
With power to grant us final deliverance after deliberations,
It is the Living Conscience
In the canvas of the mind.

The Brahmaputra is an epic story,
The atoms of our body,
It is creation itself,
Highest light.
The Brahmaputra is thought and emotion,
Word and deed,
Expression and gesture,
In divine mighty collaboration.

The Brahmaputra is Goodness,
The crown of every success,

The most blissful, blessed and beautiful.

The Brahmaputra is the shining armoured God,
In Rainbow colours,
Bathed in the essence,
Of the fragrance of myriad flowers.

The Brahmaputra is Highest Truth,
Highest Love,
Highest Beauty,
Highest bliss.

In the footnotes, Ganga wrote, 'The Brahmaputra is a trans –boundary big river, which flows through China, India and Bangladesh.'

~ ~ ~

Ganga spotted a one-horned rhino in the distant one-horned rhino territory and the adjoining green tea fields on the gliding hills, the moisture-laden sweet smelling unpolluted earth, which brought back the memories of her long-lost childhood days, the green carpet of the luxuriantly growing, youthful grass, the large number of herbs and shrubs on the large number of patches and corners, orange and plum trees and the extremely good-looking young men and women, roaming all around. Prajyotishpura was full of wonders and blemishless works of art. It was full of life but the ways of living were different. People, here, seemed to really coexist as a part of nature as opposed to the idea of man considering himself to be aloof or away from nature. Assam was an ancient land and its fair face hid several intricate beauties.

In Assam, Ganga visited the famous Kamakhya temple where tantric Shaktism was practiced. She also visited the Navagraha temple or the temple of the nine planets. Ganga also visited the multi-arts complex; Srimanta Sankaradeva Kalakshetra. Ganga also visited the Sualkuchi, the world's largest weaving village. Ganga felt proud that her country, India was the home of all the four varieties of silk: the Eri, Muga, Oak Tasar and Tasar varieties. In fact, Assam was the home of a variety of silks, golden, muga and others. She thought a lot about the conditions of the poor silk workers. Yet when she reached Sualkuchi itself and realized that several lakh of the miserable cocoons and baby silkworms in them were being killed to produce the inches of the golden silk, she felt sorry for them. Silk, to Ganga, was now a symbol - a fabric product of pain and mutilation. Ganga decided never to wear silk again in her life. Ganga wondered if it was all right to support silk production and the silk weavers or to hate it for it involved the death of the poor and voiceless insects. Suddenly Ganga realised that everything in life was filled with contradictions. There is no real, 'This' or 'That'. There is only, 'this' and 'this'.

~ ~ ~

**Ganga** had now started enjoying the vagabond life. She had been living in and out of hotels for the past several months, now. The first rays of the sun in India fell over the sunny face of Ganga in the Dong area in the Lohit district of Arunachal Pradesh. The place, Dong was situated in the north-eastern tip of the country and therefore, was always the first to receive the magnanimous rays of the sun on the bountiful mornings.

A wonderful day was spent at the Namdapha sanctuary. Ganga's guide was a highly courteous man with loads of knowledge on wildlife. His great knowledge on the subject mesmerized Ganga. After the exclusive tour was over, Ganga gave a handsome tip to the guide. The guide profusely thanked Ganga and went away, whistling an old Hindi tune and praising the Gods. Ganga came back to the entrance and collected her most precious property, Benevolence. Benevolence began to yelp in joy. It was really glad to see Ganga.

It was twilight and the night was shifting endlessly on the horizon waiting to take control of the lives of the people. The two went out for a stroll near a wooded area. Benevolence chased butterflies, reptiles and birds and was really contented to be in the company of his master, Ganga. Ganga was happy, too. Just when she was planning her next move, she heard a war cry and then before she could move, a blanket was thrown over her and four rough hands quickly lifted her. She could not see the faces of her kidnappers through the thick blanket. Benevolence was barking tremendously. He too seemed to have fallen into the net.

Ganga and Benevolence were carried quickly away into a dark forest. Ganga was pushed and disturbed by the men handling her. They appeared to have reached a clearing. The moment the blanket was taken off her, Ganga was able to see as to what was going around her. Benevolence was almost dead. Thankfully, the freshness of the cold night air saved the duo from fainting. Ganga could see rough and tough looking tribal men and women in their colourful dresses standing around a large pyre. There was a tall man who looked like the chief. He looked at Ganga with suspicious eyes. His eyebrows showed signs of dissent. 'Why have you come to disturb the forest? Don't you know that it's a sacrilege to enter our forest?' he asked in a booming voice.

For a minute, Ganga was confused. She didn't really understand as to what the man was saying. She looked a little close at all the people around her. She remembered a few pages from her history texts. Then, it struck her. 'Good heavens, these people are ancient tribal people - probably among those who still lead the life of the paleolithic men, who have had no contact with the world. We must have entered their territory by chance,' thought Ganga.

The tall young man looked at her and said to his people - 'Hus, hus, hass, hass ho hee'.

The people chanted what seemed to be an elongated version of abracadabra much to Ganga's bewilderment - 'Hus, hus, hass, hass ho, hee, Hus, hus, hass hass ho hee.'

The man-who-seemed-to be the Chief translated the words into English for her, 'My people want to cook you and eat you up.'

Ganga pleaded, 'Why must I be cooked? What have I done? I have done you all no harm except coming here, by chance. I promise to tell no one about you. You must let me go. I have a promise given to my family, which I must fulfill. I have to gain gold!'

The chief laughed loudly. The chief looked at his people and translated what she had just said to his people. 'Hus had do ga gaga,' he said. In their native language, it meant, 'She wants to gain gold.'

His people laughed with him and together chorused, '............beebee.' 'Hus had do ga ga. Bobo-bobo beebee'

The Chief said, 'They call you a stupid woman.'

Ganga seemed surprised that the people were looking so happy. She asked the chief. 'I thought that you sort of people are always moody but you look so happy and your people, too and you are all no-so-mad-except that you want to cook me'

The chief smiled and said, 'I am the only one who knows English. My people don't know your funny language.'

Ganga retorted, 'Not half as funny as your language is. I don't understand a bit.'

The smiling chief continued. 'My people are happy people and I am their happy chief. We are never sad except when someone dies or someone is sick.'

Ganga asked, 'Are you not afraid of the forest? Are you not afraid to spend the hot summers and cold winters, in darkness?'

The chief said, 'The forest is not afraid of us and we are not afraid of the forest. The forest is everything to us. We live in a state of happy fraternity, undisturbed by the happenings of the world. All of you are satanical people, who run behind materialistic desires. We people are free from desires. We spend the nights telling each other stories, the hot summers are spent on cool grass mattresses, drinking tender coconut water and water from leaves and the cold winters are spent near the fireside heat.'

Ganga said, 'Indeed, but did you say water from leaves?'

The chief said, 'Yes, you advanced humans don't know what we, the forest children have been knowing for tens of thousands of years. We know how to drink water from leaves and even from thorns.'

Ganga asked, 'We too, know a lot. Let's go. I will take all of you with me and show you how the real world, full of money and wealth looks like.'

The chief retorted. 'Money is the source of all evil and destruction! In what way has it contributed in any way to the welfare of mankind except its destruction? Money, in your world, is considered to be a measure of value but can it really measure the value of land or labour or capital or enterprise as you call it? Can money be considered as an exact measure of value?

Ganga interrupted, 'Money, Sir, is a good measure of value. The price of a commodity is determined by its demand and supply.'

The chief continued, 'That's not true. You men are evil. There is no real love or real friendship in your world. Your world is full of hypocrisy, which is nauseating. We would not want to enter it. What's in your world? You world has over-population, traffic congestions, over-crowding, over-commercialization, decline of moral values and going of man against nature. I don't think there is any modernity in all of this. Here, we have no enemies. The lion, the rabbit and the frog are all our friends. Here a man remains loyal to his woman all his life and vice-versa. Faith, that wonderful word has been mutilated by your world. We would prefer to die than enter your kingdom.'

Ganga spoke, 'Sir, you speak out of ignorance. You simply have no idea how wonderful it is to travel by trains and by planes. Even space travel is going to be within reach for the common people within its fold and here you are in this dark forest with half-naked men and women who look more like beasts, have no concept of beauty and are barbaric enough to **want...to.... feed.........on.....me'.** Her voice started to get louder and louder.

The chief loudly retorted, 'Habba! Silence! You must not speak about my people like that. My people are good and virtuous. They are morally upright. Ours is a relationship soldered by the bonds of fraternity.

There is true love in our land. Land, lust and love are markedly separate. Every man treats every woman with respect and every woman respects all the men as her brothers except of course for her man for whom she has an abiding lust. You talk about planes, trains and buses but what they really do is to separate near and dear ones. People leave behind their families and friends in search for fortune in faraway lands. There are no real emotions in your lands. Everybody is pretentious to the most unholy extent whereas we people always live together. We love each other and are one family but the rest of the world doesn't think itself to be one family but consists of individual centres of senses, passions and desires. We all have just one desire and that is the desire for the common good.'

Ganga said, 'Sir, your wife or perhaps, your lover will really adore you if you will purchase for her, a cooker and other modern gadgets like the food processor and the dish-washer. You are all missing out on all the fun and opportunities that this world provides.'

The chief smiled. 'You are right. My lover will adore me but then, I will no longer be able to adore her. All your gadgets right from the washing machines to cookers to dishwashers to refrigerators, of which my people have no knowledge about, are simply great time savers which by itself is a wonderful opportunity to rest but then my people if given these gadgets will then become like your people - lazy and full of idiosyncrasies. The women of my tribe will spend their time in gossip and not do their duties. They will be able to finish their work quickly and will indulge in character assassination of the other tribals. Do you think I will ever allow all those things to happen? My people are a happy set of people and so am I. I would always like to remain their happy chief.'

Ganga said, 'It looks like you have not really understood the beneficial effects of the television. There are several channels relaying a large number of events and programmes. Eleven men and several thousand spectators and another eleven men and their supporters make the incredible game of cricket. Your men will love the sport and also the game of football. Your women will enjoy thoroughly the sops and serials and they can laugh as much as they want and...'

~ ~ ~

The chief interrupted and said, 'And we men will have to cry. Our mothers, daughters, sisters, our wives and lovers will desert us for the sake of watching television and we will have to wait for advertisement intervals to be served our food. Now, thanks, to the non-availability of all these modern gadgets, our people are happy, busy performing their duties, getting up early in the mornings, fetching fruits and vegetables, tending the fields, sowing seeds, taking care of the plants, harvesting, taking care of their families and children, cooking their meals on the fire, dusting their homes. We spend our precious time celebrating functions, dancing, and singing and most importantly, every individual respects the other, honors traditions and lives in the greatest peace and harmony. Our clothes made of leaves and flowers make us look more beautiful than all the silk and diamonds in the world and by the way, we are naturally beautiful and need no creams, colours, chemicals and ointments to make us look beautiful. Nature is greater than the nurture that people like you are used to. God is great.'

Ganga conceded, 'Yes, you are right and what's more, there is less politics, conspiracies, jealousy, backbiting, instigation and sabotaging. We, the so called civilized human beings are truly not as good as you are but perhaps, there must be a reason for God to have created us like this. Probably, within all this imbalance and imperfection, there must be great balance and it is this secret, which has sustained the generations of men, and women who have made their footprints in this earth. Chief, your dear people are quite right in their assessments. Cook me and eat.'

The chief was flabbergasted. He quickly translated as to what Ganga had said to his people. They looked dumbfounded, too. Ganga realized that the chief and his people were trying to communicate in their native language.

Then the noise was broken by an unexpected announcement by the chief, 'We have made the decision.'

Ganga responded, 'Right. When are you going to cook me?'

The chief said, 'You are good and virtuous. You shall live. How can goodness be killed? You are not evil like the other men of your race. We shall free you and also give you a gift.' Ganga was astonished.

The chief hurried inside his hut and returned with a large bag. He handed over the bag to Ganga. Ganga peeped into the bag and discovered bars of gold and shining gems of different kinds.

It was late in the morning when Ganga reached her hotel. The sun was beginning to rise and spread its brightness among the people. The hotel manager looked suspiciously at the pretty young woman. 'Where was she last night?'

Nagaland was a most charming place with its lovely parks, gardens, hidden waterfalls and secret gifts of nature. The whole state itself was like one big beautiful park.

The Loktak lake was a beautiful floating lake. Ganga watched with awe, the Sangai deer and the antlered deer, which were grazing near the virgin waters of the lake. The deer were splendid in form and beautiful in design. They were coy and seemed to understand the world around them. It was in 1944 that the most superior, Shri Subhash Chandra Bose had first unfurled the glorious Indian flag in Moirang in Manipur. Ganga had the golden opportunity of being able to proceed to the place. Manipur had a special beauty, which Ganga was able to understand. At Moirang, Ganga enjoyed the feeling that she was in a place where one of the most important steps had been taken in the Indian freedom struggle. She recollected with happiness the lessons that she had read about the dedicated honesty and perseverance of the Indians.

~ ~ ~

Ganga travelled extensively throughout the state of Manipur. She was quite taken in by the state of the youth of the state. There existed a whole world of sad reality out there with youngsters becoming addicted to the drug habit. The shady dealings on the streets of Manipur made Ganga sad and made her to ponder over the facts that drove so many youngsters and the elderly to take to drugs. 'Is the easy availability of drugs, the main reason for this terrible state,' she wondered. Drugs were being smuggled into the state through the countries of Thailand and Burma. Ganga wished that she had the good fortune of reaching the highest echelons of power and root out this evil from the world for good.

~ ~ ~

Tripura was full of orchards, plum orchards and orange onwards. Traditional jewellery was what caught Ganga's fancy. Ganga managed to travel to the border area and saw from a distance, the broad areas of Bangladesh. The two sides of the border looked perfectly the same. The people spoke the same language, their culture was the same, and their pattern of dressing was similar. Yet, there could not be a greater difference between the two groups of people for they belonged to different countries. The benefits that the general Indian population enjoyed was much more than their counterparts in Bangladesh.

India had great natural resources, helpful people, intellectuals, tech geeks, unique identity card system, a good public distribution system better hospitals, schools and colleges, the military and technological strength to make the next quantum jump. Poverty as Preetha realised had begun reducing in India. All that it required was a great leader.

The last leg of the tour to the Northeast included a visit to Meghalaya. Meghalaya was receiving heavy rains as usual. A visit to Cherrapunji confirmed that it was indeed, the wettest spot in the world!

~ ~ ~

Ganga knew what the Indian side of Bengal had been through. India was still receiving in thousands, illegal migrants from Bangladesh. West Bengal was the intellectual hub of the nation and had produced the most learned master-scholar, the highly eulogized Rabindranath Tagore and tens of thousands of extremely talented people. To Ganga, West Bengal was special for another reason. She was an ardent follower of the tenets of the life of the greatest leader of the masses, the most outstanding standard of virtue and character, Subhash Chandra Bose. It was Subhash Chandra Bose's efforts that had seen the dawn of Indian freedom. The bespectacled image of the revolutionary had the maximum impact on Ganga and the millions of people who had walked on the path of freedom and those who were trying to emancipate themselves in ways, different from the initial struggle for freedom. To Ganga, Subhash Chandra Bose was the greatest symbol

of freedom. She had admired Bose since her childhood.
She remembered as to how, she had composed a poem
on Bose.

**'Netaji - The respected leader'**
**(A tribute to Subhas Chandra Bose, the great Indian**
**Freedom Fighter)**


*Great advocate of India's unconditional*
*Independence*
*Born in Cuttack in erstwhile Bengal province*
*A man who lived true to his own words*
*– "Only on the soil of sacrifice*
*And sufferings can we raise our National edifice."*


*He cleared the Indian Civil Services but*
*Resigned in protest. Illegitimate rule he did*
*Resist.*


*He killed his days of youth so that*
*Indian children could play in the garden of ecstatic*
*Freedom and breathe the engaging air of justice*
*Writer and editor became leader.*


*In the unforgettable Tamil leader,*
*Muthuramalinga Thevar*
*He found a staunch admirer and because of him,*
*All India Forward Bloc in the south found great favour.*

*His escape to Germany in perilous*
*Times speaks about the glory of a man, who*
*Because of an indomitable vision in his head*
*Lived light years ahead.*

*He travelled from nation to nation,*
*With dreams of his Mother's emancipation.*

*With the blessings of Rash Behari, he gave*
*New life to the Indian National Army and created*
*A separate Women's Regiment commanded by*
*A captain lady, whose name was Lakshmi.*

*He gave his youth for this country so*
*that we could live*
*Gracefully. Our Pied Piper maybe gone but his*
*Life's music lingers on. Let us give him, his due. Let us*
*Celebrate our Indian National Hero.*

Soon, Ganga was on her way to Calcutta and what a fabulous place, Calcutta was, full of intellectuals, quizzers, singers and musicians. Ganga undertook a tour of Calcutta. To Ganga, the every-day struggles and troubles of the common man in India was painful and hurting, for she had been fortunate enough to have always been a child of comfort. She had never had to carry water from miles away nor had she traveled many times in crowded buses. Ganga had never been in a position where she needed to trouble herself nor was there any pressure from any side. Ganga was a free soul who hated barriers of any sort and who didn't want the pressures of society to stifle. By now, she had learnt about how a large number of atrocities were committed in the name of tradition.

One fine evening, Ganga decided to take a long walk from her hotel. She did not know that it was a notorious area - a red light zone, where women were scantily dressed with their barbaric pimps around them, enticing every customer who was willing to fall into their net. In most cases, in the market, demand constantly out-striped supply and more and more women were drowning in a sea of evilness. It was only when she noticed that all the men in the street were looking at her that Ganga realized where she was and she darted from the area with her dog in tow. 'What a close escapade that I have had,' thought Ganga and patted Benevolence and rewarded him with a large number of milk biscuits. Ganga felt really unhappy for the women who had been caught by the clutches of the evil and she was grateful to her faithful dog, which had been with her through thick and thin.

Ganga hurried back to her hotel with its colourfully lit lights, busy corridors and conference halls where intellectuals met and discussed. Ganga was mentally distressed and wanted to know was as to why the Government were not making real progress is helping the poor trapped women in finding alternative employment.

~ ~ ~

The next day, Ganga went about seeing the other side of Calcutta with its bustling bazaar, jewellery shops, sweet shops, theaters, dramas, dancers and artists. She even meet a couple of painters and was pleasantly surprised to find out how committed they were. She also saw the river Ganga flowing below the famous Howrah Bridge.

Ganga realized that Bengal was a beautiful land notwithstanding its several defects. Ganga wanted the same Bengal sans its unhygienic environment, overcrowding, overpopulation, unsanitary conditions, bad water supply and recurrent electricity shortages.

~ ~ ~

Since childhood, Ganga had always wanted to visit the Andaman and Nicobar Islands. Ganga arrived at the Indian Airlines Office in Calcutta. It was when she was there seeking details about the air fare to the Andamans, when a knowledgeable-looking woman at the Information Counter told her, 'Madam, look there are concessional air tickets to the islands,' showing her the brochures on the same subject. Ganga's eyes quickly ran over the main contents of the brochures. The Maharaja had introduced a new scheme. The first hundred bookings on each flight to the Andamans in the Economy class would have to pay just 50%. 'What a bonanza!' thought Ganga. There were places on Ganga's agenda including the beautiful red coral stretches, beaches, monuments like the cellular jails, barren islands and all. She went to the islands on her own in a boat which she hired from the tourism department but when she went there, she found a large number of tourists already there. Ganga felt betrayed and angry. She thought that she would be able to enjoy the beauty of the quiet volcano in solitude and was thoroughly disappointed to see the large crowds of badly dressed and behaving tourists who were throwing eatables, leftovers and plastic objects on the region away from the volcano's mouth. The barren islands were a group of pristine islands with traces of lava on the ground far away from the mouth of the volcano but the barren islands were not barren. There were small groups of tribals who lived there, too in their little round huts made of leaves and who looked with curiosity at the tourists. The volcano, which wrecked havoc years ago, seemed quiet and friendly with no trace of evil and not even the intention of evil.

~ ~ ~

From the barren islands, Ganga returned to the main islands. She went to see the most famous, rather infamous cellular jail where those who had struggled for the freedom of the country, India had to struggle for their lives. Many of the great freedom fighters had been hanged, tortured and mutilated in the grim surroundings of the ghastly cellular jail. The jail, a creation of the superb but evil genius of the British mind had been a witness to the most violent tortures, cruelties and pain to the Indian freedom fighters. Ganga began to dwell on the topic, 'Perhaps, some great grand father or grand uncle of mine had died here,' and almost instantaneously, she could sense some kind of communication link being formed instantaneously with the hidden and dead spirits of the place. Ganga became so excited that she almost shook. Suddenly, an apparition appeared in front of Ganga's eyes. The face of an unrecognizable woman appeared. The woman looked very young and her face looked unhappy and miserable. She spoke, 'My child, I am your great grandmother's sister's daughter. I died young. I joined the freedom struggle on the call of the inimitable Subhash Chandra Bose who told us to give the country, our blood and in return, take back freedom. I joined the freedom struggle and rallied support for it from all sides in our native village near Meerut. Freedom came much later but I was gone. I married a man in Singapore where the women ranks were stationed. The two of us lost of our lives in delivering this land to freedom. Our support might have been small but it was significant, I believe. For the first time, in the history of India, women began to fight for the rights of the people. Bose was our pillar of support and thousands of us lay down our lives for the great leader. In Cellular jail my husband and I both contracted a deadly disease, the name of which, I struggle to say, not because I know not its name but I fear that should I say, then you might not love me.

Ganga replied, 'If you love me so much, then it is my abiding duty to love you, too. Love is always reciprocal. Just tell me, one thing, what happened to your children?' The apparition spoke again, 'My child,

I left my two children, very young and tender under the care of a Japanese couple. I knew that the Japanese have a strong set of family values and I believed that they would provide reasonable care for my children. Perhaps, they were well, perhaps, they died but that was years ago.'

Ganga spoke wistfully, 'Perhaps, I will meet my cousin, your descendant somewhere, sometime.'

The apparition spoke, 'Yes, anything can happen anywhere, any place. I never imagined that you would come here but my special sense, which only ghosts possess, told me that you would come and I would meet a relation, again.'

Ganga smiled again. 'Are you happy that we have won freedom?'

The apparition spoke again, 'Yes, of course, but things have worsened after freedom has been won. There is corruption, misdistribution of income and wealth, inequalities in wages and prices, inflation, poverty, unemployment, sexual exploitation, rapes, female foeticides, female infanticides, eve teasing and all. I am a disappointed ghost.' Survival is the key to good fortune and prosperity. When work is worship, play is useless. The trip to the Andamans, thus, proved to be fateful and nostalgic for Ganga.

When Ganga stepped into the train to go to Orissa, she could hear many people speaking in a sweet but half-recognizable tongue. She thought what she was hearing sounded a bit like Bengali but it was not Bengali. It was the Oriya language, which had fascinated Ganga. It was only much later that Ganga recognized that Oriya, the language spoken by several people in Orissa had several shades of Bengal and Telugu.

Bhubaneshwar was a most remarkable city with its perfectly laid out roads and parks. The beauteous city was the single-handed contribution of Le Corbusieur, the architect par excellence who had also designed the city of Chandigarh. There were many parks (as Ganga found to her great happiness!) Where one could sit, stand, read or simple stare at the gloriously beautiful creepers, bushes, grasses, leaves, branches and trees. Though the month was March, the water, which flowed out of the taps of Ganga's hotel, was still very cold and the weather was rather colourful with varying shades of chillness and warmth. Ganga was able to go to see the famed Lingaraja temple. It was a very tall structure and it seemed to touch the sky. The great and wonderful structure evoked and kindled in Ganga, the desire to reach great, great heights and to be a towering personality. The Lingaraja temple was a very well sculpted and ornately decorated structure. The Rajarani temple was also a beautiful structure. The temple shone like a crystal in the moonlit and well lighted site on the night when Ganga went to see the temple. The temple was closed at nighttime.

From Bhubaneshwar, Ganga took a tourist mini-bus where once again, she had to sit with twenty-five other tourists to go to Puri. Puri was a bustling place where the old and new seemed to coexist with satisfaction. On one hand, it was full of penury, dust and dirt. On the other hand, Puri was full of holiness, throbbing peace amidst great noise, ancience and old temples including its most famous temple, the Jagannath Temple. Puri was one of the four Hindu Dhams or places of pilgrimage for the Hindus. The darsan of Lord Jagannath and his consort filled Ganga's heart with pure happiness and ecstasy. The bulging eyes of the dominant lord seemed to be taking up all the pressures of the world without much ado. The stinking ill maintained toilets of Puri, into one of which Ganga had the unfortunate necessity to go made Ganga wonder as to what the states were doing with the funds allotted for the maintenance of the hygiene of its cities. Ganga was flabbergasted but of course, there was not much that she could do. It was to Ganga's good fortune that she did not contract any disease.

Konark was the next destination. Konark was one of the few temples in the world to boast of a Sun-temple. The Sun God seemed all-powerful with his seven magnificent horses and superb chariot. He seemed ready to fly. The wheels of the chariot were very ornately designed. Ganga brought one or two of the replicas of the wheels in semi-precious stone Ganga drank fresh coconut juice from a coconut, which she brought from a vendor. The month of March and the accompanying salubrious climate seemed very soothing and it rested every tourist who came there. At the picturesque and poignant village of Pipli, Ganga bought bags, purses and others for her family's female members. The mirror work on the cloth seemed an absolute must for the fashion-conscious and it was seductive enough to attract the stares of all the people in the street.

As Ganga went deeper and deeper into the state of Orissa, she found that it had more than just temples and forests, for hidden in the grand canopy of prosperity were a large number of impoverished people who ate boiled mango seeds and leaves.

~ ~ ~

Ganga heard a loud sound of mourning in one Mehboob Nagar's lost villages. Mehboob Nagar is one of the drier districts of South India. When the quirk of fate had Ganga stepping into the courtyard of a house, there, she realised that there was a huge crowd, which had already gathered there. Women were beating their chests and the little children were crying out aloud. Ganga, who was among that crowd that particular day asked one amongst the crowd, 'What happened? Why is everybody crying?' The man who had been asked the question stared so hard back at Ganga that she felt sick and wanted to get out of the place. Then, the man replied, 'What you have just witnessed is one of the several deaths take place regularly here, in Andhra Pradesh. The man, who died, committed suicide. He was a young farmer. I am farmer, too and we face the same problems. He was neck-deep-in-debts. We just can't pay back.' Ganga asked, 'Won't the government support you?' The farmer replied, 'Yes, of course but only sometimes. That happens rarely. We are at the mercy of the local moneylenders who tantalize us each day!'

Ganga said, 'How dreadful! It is very distressful to think that we pay so much attention to industry at the cost of agriculture. In fact, you people deserve more subsidies, free water, free electricity, free manure, high yielding varieties of seeds and other incentives. After all, you people work the hardest.'

As she was going around the site, Ganga noticed that a man looking for something in the pharmacy. By now, Ganga knew that the pharmacist was working hand-in-glove with the men who were committing suicide. Ganga followed the man who had bought something, who had hidden it and who was walking hurriedly towards his destination, presumably his home. Ganga hurried up and caught up with the young man. 'What's that you are having with you?' she asked in English. The poor man looked flabbergasted. He didn't understand a word of what seemed to him as a very queer language but when Ganga gesticulated pointing out to his hands, the man helplessly opened up. His shivering hands held out a dose of poison. Ganga scowled so much that the man dropped his packet and ran.

Ganga ran after him. It seemed so weird, to be chasing a man on a hot afternoon. To Ganga, it was a matter of utmost importance to save the man. 'Why would anybody want to die?' she wondered. The totally terrified runner called aloud his neighbour to come and rescue him from this woman, who was chasing him!

The man's intellectual neighbour who knew English explained the complicated circumstances in which the man was.

Ganga countered, 'So, you mean to tell me that you are willing to die for a sum of ten thousand rupees! Here, I will give you the ten thousand which has bothered you so much and another two thousand to make you live,' said Ganga, handing over the sum of money to the stunned man. The man's happiness knew no bounds. He took the crisp and magical notes in his hands, mumbled 'thank you' and ran away. Ganga soon tracked nine more men in the village who were reeling under debts. One lakh precious rupees were gone in a couple of magnanimous minutes but Ganga felt proud and happy. The astonished men asked Ganga, 'Who are you? Are you an angel?'

Ganga had just seen one of the several troubles that India was facing, the problem of debt. Slowly, the realization of multiple Indias grew in Ganga's heart. She was beginning to see the rich India, the poor India, the sick India, the healthy India, the disciplined India, the wild India, the old India, the young India, the dead India and the vibrant India.

~ ~ ~

Tamilnadu was a big world. It was full of diversity. The land was blessed. At Kanchipuram, Ganga was able to go and see the large number of temples, which had been built by the Pallavas. The Pallavas had been great kings and they had established their supremacy over

Kanchipuram as well as Mamallapuram or the present day Mahabalipuram. Ganga was able to visit both the places and was wonderstruck at the capacity and talents of the great Tamil people. She was astonished at the precision and clarity of the ancient Indians in the execution of gigantic temples of extraordinary geometrical beauty. They were veterans of Temple sculpture. There was music and dance on the walls of the structures. All the structures from the gopuram to the sanctum sanctorum were exquisitely constructed. Ganga marveled and marveled at every nuance and turn. In front of the Big Brihadeeshwara temple at Tanjore, Ganga felt helpless and weak. What a colossal structure it was and how very extraordinary! It felt like standing before the pyramids at Giza, though Ganga had never been to Egypt. It was natural for Ganga to be feeling stunned.

After all, time and again, man has realized his own strengths and weaknesses only in comparison with the natural wonders such as the oceans or mountains or forests or animals like the lion or with manmade marvels such as the marvelously beautiful Fatehpur Sikri or the Pyramids of Egypt. Ganga experienced a similar inner awakening after seeing the stupendous Brihadeeshwara temple.

~ ~ ~

At Velankanni, near the coast facing the breathtaking Bay of Bengal, Ganga worshiped at the shrine of Virgin Mary. She found the land and its language to be ancient and classical. Just as everywhere else - people were good, bad, noble and ignoble. Ooty, Kodaikanal and Yercaud offered her glimpses of the hill life, the beauty of flowers and the hidden joys of nature. She ended her trip to Tamilnadu with a trip to Rameswaram, an island on the Bay of Bengal connected to the mainland of India by means of the Pamban Bridge. The place was intrinsically connected to the mythological story of the 'Ramayana'. In fact, Ganga heard from the people there that the bridge built by the Vanaras or the monkey gods for the movement of Lord Rama and his army to Sri Lanka to fight the demon king 'Ravana' was still lying undisturbed under water. Ganga recalled with pride that Rameshwaram was also the birth place of Dr.A.P.J. Abdul Kalam, the President of the Indian Republic. At Kanyakumari, Ganga saw the intermingling of the three seas, the Bay of Bengal, the Arabian Sea and the Indian Ocean and she could hear the gentle breathing of the virgin goddess.

# CHAPTER
# *Twenty Three*
## *Nearing the End of a Long Journey*

The captivating backwaters and the greenish-blue sea brought about an exciting plethora of feelings in Ganga. In Ganga's opinion, Kerala was a small state but with a mind blowing array of incredibly fascinating arts, cultural aspects, music, dance and martial arts.

**'Ode to Kerala**

*Decked up in the fragrance of a million*
*myriad hues of forest flowers*
*Steeped in verdant mysteries of ancient history*
*Blessed by the oceans and the seas*
*South Indian beauty beyond compare*
*First born of God's earthy children*
*Born from the compassion of The Heavens*
*Looked after by passion incarnate nature*
*Soaked in splendorous waterfalls and rivers*

*Bathed in the warmth of surreptitious sunlight*
**Kerala**, *with one foot in the waters and*
*the other on the sands*
*Land of Mahabali, great asura king in*
*the Matsya Purana*
*Sent to the netherworld by Vamana -*
*Vishnu Avatara*
*Backwaters stretching to the length of imagination*
*Into prurient human hearts*
*Muse of poets.....*
*Blessed by water in every form and girth*
*River water- falls....rains...and sea!*
*The land of elephants, coconuts, bananas, roses red*
*Nature has given this flamboyant woman,*
*Its finest!'*

~ ~ ~

It was a warm April afternoon when Ganga caught the train to Karnataka. Karnataka was the gem of India with its unspoilt natural splendour and extremely good-looking people. It was a blend of tradition and modernity and it was the home of the nouveau riche who had made fast bucks in the software industry. Mysore was also full of palaces and gardens. Ganga had the desire to visit the Mysore Maharaja palace and she fulfilled the desire to visit the palatial structure. It was full of artifacts and treasures of unparalleled excellence. Ganga just sat on the cool floor of the palace and noted with marvel, the superb round paintings on the ceilings. 'How could the artisans paint such beautiful works of arts on the ceilings which are so high', wondered Ganga. The Mysore ruling family, the Wodeyar family was a most respected family. It was a curse that had destroyed the line of heirs. They Mysore Maharaja, whoever had been power, never had any male heir. It was, therefore, not a direct genealogical line that ruled Mysore. The Chamundeshwari temple facing the eastern direction atop the hill was one of the most important places that Ganga had the privilege of visiting. The mother Chamundeshwari seemed to be blessing all of Mysore with her divine presence. The Ranganathitoo bird sanctuary with its large number of birds was a unique attraction to Ganga who felt one with the birds and with all the creations of God. Ganga felt that perhaps the birds and animals did not lack any sense but were probably blessed with more than six senses. At Belur and Halebed, Ganga saw the huge temples but was impressed with the holistic approach of the artisans who had constructed the temple. In fact, Ganga was thoroughly impressed with all that she saw.

~ ~ ~

Goa was Ganga's next stop. Goa had not been a part of the Indian territory till the nineteenth day of December, 1961 when Goa was liberated from Portuguese rule and made a composite Union territory which included Daman and Diu. The latter got delineated into a separate union territory and Goa became a State in 1987. The history of the state was truly inspiring and Ganga could see the impact of the former Portuguese rule on the people. Even the way, the people spoke had traces of Portuguese impact. Their Konkani and Marathi were distinct and beautifully clumsy. Ganga toured the entire State traveling by bus, taxis and private auto-rickshaws.

At Mormugoa, the major port in the State, Ganga saw several ships standing in the harbour. She was fascinated by the smell of the sultry waters, the noisy crowds and the constant life force, which seemed to get regenerated from time to time from somewhere. A large portion of the exports and imports was carried by the seas and not by airways or railways as people thought. The sea seemed magical and almost seemed to be wooing Ganga. Ganga thoroughly enjoyed the chill evening air by the sea and ate the popcorns and chilly chips, which she had brought from the young boy vendors. In the evenings, she would stare at the ships moving at a distance. Ganga wanted to see as to how a ship would look from the inside but she did not know a soul in the shipping network and thereby could not satisfy her compelling desire. Satiation of a desire gives strength to further hopes and all of Ganga's hopes of seeing the internal layout of a ship were put to sleep. Ganga visited almost all the main towns of Panaji, Margao, Vasco, Mapusa and Pouda.

Goa was the glorious land of beaches and sun-kissed vast sandy stretches. Vasco on the western coast of Goa on the coast of the Arabian see was full of drug peddlers whom Ganga hated totally. What Ganga did not know what that even the police were hand in-gloves with the drug peddlers. Most of these drugs were arriving from the drug-cultivating areas of Pakistan and Afghanistan. In the case of delinquents who were committing crimes under the influence of drugs, instead of sending the children-criminals to reformatory schools, in most cases the police were freeing them as soon as possible, often within hours of the arrests. This was because, as Ganga did not know, the police themselves were afraid of facing charges of committing atrocities against children by the Magistrates before whom the police had the duty of producing the children in the courts. Of course, mostly, the police were never cruel to children but unfortunately; the Magistrates were always the ones to keep suspecting. They were often the ones, who committed more crimes.

It had been almost a month Ganga was walking alone, one evening, to her place in Vasco with Benevolence when she was intercepted by a couple of men who looked like gangsters. The gangsters tried to outrage her modesty but were bitten by Benevolence. However by then, they had already beaten up Ganga. Ganga was left to die on the road but then Ganga did not die. She dragged her swollen and out of place body to the nearest clinic. The nurse who saw the poor bloodied woman quickly brought the stretcher and made Ganga to lie on the stretcher. The nurse deftly moved the stretcher with Ganga on it to the doctor in charge of the clinic. Benevolence bounced with the quick moving stretcher with his master on it. The nurse did not mind the four begged mongrel's behaviour and on the contrary appeared to be much impressed with the animal's sense of loyalty. The doctor asked the nurse, 'Who is this?' The nurse replied, 'Whoever it is, that's a matter that we could check out later. This woman needs help, doctor.' Ganga recovered. Soon, she was on her way out of the hospital. She profusely thanked the doctor and his nurse for treating her so well. Her worthy benefactors were very rare personalities and worthy persons are always rewarded well for their deeds. Ganga paid the doctor a handsome fee.

In Delhi where Ganga had studied, most of her friends had sworn by the virtues of Bombay. Bombay to them was a land of fantasy, where dreams changed into reality, where their screen Gods and goddesses lived. To many other people, Bombay was the greatest place of cricket, a real heaven for cricket enthusiasts, the home of no smaller a man than the genius Sachin himself. Ganga had never been the one to believe easily or everything that people said and was always a querent even before her own realization. Ganga would go on and on asking questions and not resting until she found her answers. Even in her sleep, her mind and dreams coalesced and kept provoking her to find all the answers to the questions of life but one thing was perfectly clear to Ganga that no matter, how provocative men were going to be, nature would never allow them to know all its mysteries.

Landing in the busy Bombay railway station itself seemed like a dream. There were coolies or porters almost running with luggage and their customers catching up with them, an odd vendor, here, there, who wanted to sell just about everything from popcorns to omelettes to newspapers to poetry to encyclopaedias. People were eating, hurrying, talking hurriedly, talking quietly, praying, crying, laughing, helping, bugging, bubbling, trouncing, racing, foot-tapping, gazing at the rat-infested urine-smelling railway tracks, singing, gazing into mirrors, self-conscious women continuously applying make-up on their faces etcetera. It was a crazy world. Bombay bore no semblance of sanity. It seemed the repository of insaneness. The Bombay city is a city of around one hundred and fifty seven square kilometers with a big population. The Home of Bollywood and Business was a very bustling place, indeed!

~ ~ ~

Ganga dragged her feet through the screaming crowds. Ganga was feeling claustrophobic and wanted to breathe in the fresh air of June morning. Nature did not disappoint Ganga to a great extent. There had been some mild showers in the morning and there was reasonable moisture in the air, which was sufficient to bring the colour back into our young traveler's checks.

Now, Ganga decided that it was time for some learning. Ganga had wasted enough time sightseeing and roaming. She wanted to be something useful and fruitful. Living in the world of information and information linkages, Ganga knew that it would be the right thing to do to learn computers. So, she enrolled in a computer course to learn a bit about Information Technology. It wasn't the course which interested Ganga but also the ambience and friends. Tia was one of Ganga's friends in the computer technology training institution. Every time Ganga would try to strike a conversation with a new person, she would invariable succeed but with Tia, the results were always far from satisfying. Ganga tried speaking with Tia and Tia again and again. Slowly, the shy and small girl opened up.

'So, where are you from" asked Ganga.

'From Manipur,' replied Tia and stopped short of saying anything further.

By now, Ganga became hugely interested to know more about Tia and wanted Tia to speak further. Just as their conversation began her computer teacher called the girls to get back into class for the classes were about to start. Their conversation broke off.

Later on, after many days Tia opened up. 'I have not spoken to many persons in several years. I came to Mumbai six years back after completing my twelfth class back home. I didn't bring anything with me except my mother's jewels, which she gave to me in the hope that I would do something worthwhile with it. I haven't seen my father since I was six. He is a lecherous man, adulterous and scheming. He left my mother when I just a child and my mother got involved with another man, soon after. My home in Manipur was like hell. Both mother and step- father were drug addicts and sometimes used to smoke in front of me. They used to use syringes, which they often exchanged with each other. They used to send me, a young and pretty girl to fetch their drugs for them. I used to feel sick and nauseated. Ganga interrupted, 'How could you tolerate such nonsense? I feel very sorry for you.' Ganga put her right arm gently over Tia's shoulders. Tia cried openly like a child.

Ganga was simultaneously thinking about her own life. 'My parents are so good, so virtuous and I did not even listen to my mother when she asked me to not to leave her. I didn't show the slightest consideration for anyone, man or animal. I have lived these eight months solely for myself, enjoying myself and seeing the world. Why haven't I even thought of others? Why have I never displayed the motherly or sisterly love for anyone like a woman should have even before? My parents gave me everything I wanted even when I didn't know how to express as to what I wanted. Education, money, wealth and happiness have flooded my life and never even knew!'

Ganga's thoughts broke off as Tia continued. 'Has it been long since you came here?' Ganga replied in the negative. 'Oh! It's been just a couple of days.'

Tia spoke. 'You just don't know about this city, Bombay. It would be hypocritical to say that this city is full of freedom and goodness for it has its fair share of fallacies. Don't tell anybody any of secrets that I have revealed so far and will reveal further. Ganga, Bombay cheated me with its false pomp, glamour and grandeur. There is more unfaithfulness, adultery, lecherousness and permissiveness here than elsewhere in India. I came here, thinking that all human beings were like my brothers and sisters but it was only after I came here that I realized that there were not many who shared my perspective.'

Ganga replied determinedly, 'I perfectly share your perspective.'

'My child was born out of wedlock,' said Tia. Ganga felt dazed.

Ganga almost screamed, 'Good heavens, who shall save you?'

Tia answered, 'I don't quite know, Ganga'.

Ganga asked, 'How did it all happen?' Actually, when I came here, I didn't know anybody and I pledged some of my mother's jewels. With the money, I took a small room on rent. The owner had a son who used to come to collect rent from me. The young man often sympathized with me and made me repeat my old story to him. I took him into my confidence. I was a fool to believe him but I think this delusion possesses every hapless, moneyless, less educated or uneducated woman. I became a victim to his tantalizing charms. He was a very good-looking guy but he was not a brave man. He left me in that swollen state and ranaway. It's been one problem after another. Just around six months ago, my child turned one year and I wanted to be of use to my young son. I have got a job as an assistant; a peon in an office and with the money that I have saved; I have enrolled for the course, here. Dear Ganga, I envy you. You are so pure and so loving.'

Tia was speaking, 'You know, Ganga, there are many problems that our world is facing today. You know, Ganga, a society is not built over a day but over years and is the result of multiple interactions. A good society will result when there a good influences and an evil one will result when there are evil influences. I was a personal victim of society. You know, Ganga, there are hundreds of young boys and girls, some as young as six and seven who are all the victims of abuse. Drug addiction is a huge problem in our society. The value systems are dying. I wish someone could save them. There are drug lords and drug suppliers who make young children to steal money and materials to pay them for these horrid drugs. I saw my own young brother die of drug addiction, in fact, of heartbreak. My Bobo stole money and a radio from our neighbour in Manipur to pay for drugs. He was handed over to the Police. He died in custody some say of a heartbreak, some say of hunger, some say, because of withdrawal symptoms. All the same, I am angry with society and with our governments. Could they have not saved my brother? Can't they provide for allowances to housewives and for unemployment doles to the unemployed? My brother was just seven, when he died!' Tia broke into wild tears.

Ganga knew that she would have to be strong in order to provide strength do her friend.

Tia said, 'Ganga, this computer education has drained my resources. I want to study further and find a better job in order to fend for my child and myself. We are poor and the world isn't kind to those who are poor. You know Ganga; I don't even know how to proceed further for my studies. I don't know the method. I haven't made a friend in years. You are my new friend. Have by any chance, any idea of how to go about in order to pursue-college education?'

Ganga replied, 'Of course, I do for I have been through the process myself. First, you will have to apply for the course. For that, you will have to choose a course, buy the application form from the concerned college with the period stipulated by the authorities, fill in the details and submit the completed application form within the stipulated time after which you receive your hall ticket to work the exam/the entrance exam. Once you have cleared them, you can pay the fees and join the course.'

Tia replied, 'Thank you, so much. I neither have the money or the energy to do the course, right now'.

Ganga said, 'But you must, Tia, I will see you, tomorrow morning at eleven, here in the juice shop. Bring all your academic certificates with you tomorrow and I will do what has to be done. Tia replied, 'Yes Ganga, I trust you. See you tomorrow.' The two sister-like friends bid each other goodbye and departed with the promise that they would meet the next day. The night was a long one for both. Ganga was thinking hard the whole night and Tia could hardly sleep with excitement. She constantly patted her baby who was fast asleep. He looked beautifully angelic due to the inexplicable smile on his face.

At eleven, the next day, the two friends met. Ganga checked whether her friend had brought the necessary academic credentials with her. She almost pulled Tia into an autorickshaw and directed the driver to proceed to Sophia College. It was a women's college. The auto-driver was happy to proceed to the chosen destination. He knew that he would have the chance to go right into the campus and look at all the pretty, blushing sweet young things without being seen. He told the two friends that he would wait for them and take them back in his autorickshaw.

The Sophia College was a lovely college with its laws and imposing buildings.

Ganga entered the front office of the college and asked them about the application forms.

The lady at the counter stumbled for words and said. 'But, ma'am, the application forms were given a long time back in April. The applicants who applied are currently in the process of being selected. The interview days start from the 20$^{th}$ June.'

Ganga mumbled some gibberish to herself. Ganga wanted to get Tia, a seat in this institution of excellence.

Ganga spoke again, 'Ma'am may I speak to the Principal of this College? I would like to fix up an appointment with her, please?'

The secretary replied with a spiteful face, 'And what name shall I give to the Principal, Miss….'

Ganga responded immediately - 'Miss Ganga!'

The secretary responded, 'Perhaps, she will be able to spare two minutes for you, the next month, around the middle of July.'

Ganga pleaded with the woman, 'Madam, kindly consider this as an urgent case and show mercy'. The secretary concurred. 'All right, the day-after-tomorrow, around five and five forty-five in the evening, before the Principal leaves, she could meet you.'

Ganga thanked her profusely.

On the appointed day, Ganga took Tia with her to meet the Principal of the reputed college. Tia was all smiles and vibrant.

Ganga entered the Principal's chamber with soft-footed Tia who almost entered the well-decorated room like the soft breeze. The Principal did not smile at them. Ganga was asked to take a seat. Tia sat on the adjoining seat. Ganga explained the case to the Principal. The Principal slowly opened up and finally smiled. 'I have never known anybody like you and I can definitely say, in the truest faith that I never will'. The Principal called up her secretary and asked to look into the details of the case. The Principal spoke to the higher authorities to take Tia's as a special case. In a matter of hours, an application form was issued, filled and submitted. Tia attended the interview and passed the test and was granted admission. She was asked to pay the fees, which amounted to the sum of five thousand, a small sum for Ganga and a splendid beginning for Tia. The next, Tia withdrew from the computer course and paid the fees of her new college course for the first semester using the refunded sum.

She told Ganga, 'I have paid for just one Semester but I have three years to go and I have to give up my job. What do I do?'

Ganga surprised her friend by presenting her with a cheque. Tia was so totally taken in by the joy of the sudden train of events that she hugged Ganga and thanked her profusely. Ganga had given Tia, a new life. Tia was born again.

Ganga was soon becoming quite disinterested in the computer course with all its syntaxes and jargon. She decided that since she was already reasonably adept in the lessons, she could learn the rest of the course from the course material and there would be no reason as to why she ought to lose her time. There are two more states and several more union territories to covered in just two more months. August 15$^{th}$ beckoned her.

It was a long backbreaking journey from Bombay to Aurangabad. At three hundred and ninety two kilometers away from Bombay, Aurangabad was a far-off destination but it would present to Ganga, a fine taste like lovely old wine in its ancient and ageless structures. The monsoons had arrived in Maharashtra and were beating the windows of her old bus with the power of relentless energy. Ganga as well as several of her co-passengers had to close the shutters to prevent the waters from moistening her clothes or herself. The bus meandered through the hilly terrains in slow rhythmic pattern for the engine was old and the man who drove the engine was even older but all this suited Ganga and she began to slumber. As she began to sleep, her dreams and memories collided and she thought, 'Mumbai or Bombay is the largest textiles market in the world. It is also the largest film city in the world but what about Aurangabad? It was the seat of power of the ancient Mughal Empire? And then she began to dream about the Taj, the Agra Fort, the Fatehpur Sikri, the beaches of Goa, the musical bells of the temples of Tamilnadu, the divineness of the God's own country and then it all began to get fuzzy and soon Ganga was fast asleep unaware of the parading hills, the rocking bus, the noisy babies on board, the men who ogled at her and the women around who were feeling jealous about her richness. With faithful Benevolence-brother around, there were no fears to stalk her and no anguish to share. Ganga slept like a innocent baby sleeping in its mother's arms. What a lovely exhilarating feeling it was and the cold rains calming the heat of the sun and all was well under the sky.

Ganga did not feel too pleased with Aurangabad. The place was quite polluted with several factories having set up their base there. Ganga stayed in a room leased from the Tourism Department. The first place that Ganga visited in the quaint place of Aurangabad was Bibi Ka Maqbara. The sight that met Ganga's eyes when she reached the place was quite unexpected and Ganga was not well prepared at all. Since Ganga did not hire any guide to show her ground the place, there was an initial stupefaction. The place, the monument looked exactly like the Taj Mahal at Agra. It was only later that Ganga came to know that the Bibi Ka Maqbara was actually the burial place of Aurangazeb's first wife, Rabia-ud-Durani. No wonder, the son wanted to outshine his father but could not do the same. Ganga kept traveling hanging on to the tangy deliciousness of the fleeting moments She traveled fast and adjusted her responses and feelings to the fast changing scenarios. Ganga knew that she had limited time to enjoy whatever beauty lay around her before she could get back, home.

At the Panchakki or water wheel, Ganga saw the beautiful water reservoir built by Malik Ambar, the architect of Auragazeb's dream city, Aurangabad. In those days in the bygone generation, the water wheel had been used to grind the grains for the travelers especially the large number of pilgrims. 'How fortunate, they must have been,' thought Ganga. 'The people would have lucky having such wise and caring rulers who provided them wells, water, rest-houses to the people's satisfaction. 'The best part was that in the yesteryears, the relationship between the ruler and his people was the relationship between a father and his children. Unfortunately, things were changed with people coming to power for mere aggrandizement.

At around fifty kilometers away from Aurangabad was Maheshmal. It was a lovely hill resort and one of those few places in Maharashtra, which were clean. Ganga had a whale of a time in Maheshmal listening to the 'coo-coos' of the birds, the 'chee-chees' of monkeys, the lazy sound of moving water with the oars in the water from the boat, magnificent views, quietness of unparalleled proportions, the smell of fragrant flowers and dusky goats, sheep and dogs. Ganga thoroughly enjoyed the clear place. Fortunately for her, her co-tourists were friendly and well mannered. Due to her constant interaction with the local guides, local people and children, vendors and all, Ganga's fluency in the local language, Marathi increased.

From, Ganga traveled to Ellora. The journey to Ellora was through hilly segments and caves. The journey seemed not to a place in real time but in some strange timeliness. As the bus stopped near the caves, all the tourists got down from the bus. There were many, who were conversing excitedly about the caves and what they had heard about them. Soon, Ganga could hear the excited voices of the tourists discussing about whatever the guides were speaking about.

As Ganga listened, her eyes shifted from the object of explanation in the rocks to the explanation and back and forth. As Ganga learnt, there were thirty-four caves in all, representing and taking inspiration from three different religions and all of them in the very same place. The guide and the tourists first headed in the southern direction of the structures. It was full of Buddhist Caves or caves dedicated to Buddhism and to see Buddha along with the Bodhisattvas.

The twelve caves were all superbly crafted structures. The sixth cave was what really struck a chord with Ganga, herself a Hindu. This cave along the tenth cave was extremely fortunate to house the images of the Buddha and the Hindu Gods. Vishwakarma, the incomparable architect of the devas had his image in the sixth cave, fifth cave and tenth cave were unique for blending the essences of Buddhism and Hinduism in the cauldron of cultural exchange, this, a thousand and five hundred years back. Ganga who lived in the twenty-first century could not believe if what she was seeing was real (or not), yet the striking perfection in the structures astonished Ganga and proved them to be genuine. The cave of Vishwakarma was both a monastery and a temple for the Buddhists. Mostly, it was the monks who stayed in the basaltic caves away from the mad crowds.' Both Hinduism and Buddhism preach tolerance and peace.' This, Ganga realized, was quite the same as the concept of Ahimsa of Jainism and the concept of forgiveness chiefly enunciated in the books of Christianity. Different religions had drawn several of their concepts and beliefs from the other religions and faiths.

The Ellora experience was proving to be an exciting one for Ganga. The Vishwakarma cave was a truly wondrous sight with its sculptures, which looked like dwarfs sporting instruments and creating wonderful music. Ganga could well imagine how the monks would have felt in the wonderful calmness of the caves. The caves were ethereal and as Ganga walked through the caves and from one cave to the other, she could sense that she was experiencing one of the more sublime moments of human existence. Ganga felt as if she had gone back a thousand years. She could now understand how much the world had changed with its people now wanting noise and disturbance, a feature completely different from the wants of the people of the bygone generation who wished for quietness and peace. Ganga understood that the world was standing in the zone of transition.

The greatest of the thirty and four caves of Ellora was the cave number sixteen. Ganga was stunned to see its marvelous structure. After all, as the guide had correctly put it, the only equivalent of the Ellora's Kailasa Cave was the most superbly executed structure, the frighteningly majestic, Raja Raja Chola temple or the Brihadeeshwara temple. The entire cave had been carved out of a single block of rock. The Kailasa temple was a most brilliant piece of architectural wonder, which had carvings, made of human strength on the walls of the cave. Diverse pieces of history and legends such as the Ramayana, Mahabharata had been effectively retained for the coming generations in the spirit of the stone for all to marvel and to invoke the desire to excel. The entire carving and chiseling process was a tribute to the excellence of human effort and the grand process had been carried over the years. It had taken almost a century to complete the monolith.

The guide continued and questioned the tourists. 'How do you think the structure was carved out, from the base to the top?'

One bright tourist concurred, 'Of course, that's how any structure is constructed. You can't make a structure out of the air. You need to have a foundation for a superstructure.'

The guide interrupted and said, 'Now, that's what makes this structure so wonderful. You could imagine how the pilgrims and monks would have built. Most surprisingly, this entire structure was carved from the top. The architects and sculptors first worked at the top, then on the sides and then they proceeded down below. The huge marvel is a representation of the Himalayas, to be precise, Kailasa, the Lord Shiva's home in the mountains.'

Ganga marveled at the elaborately done structure and equally marveled at the guide who knew so much about these caves and who had spent his learning years at this wonderful site and who looked a little like the monks himself. Ganga enquired from the guide as to what his religion was. The guide said he was a quasi Christian-Hindu-Muslim-Jain-Buddhist! Ganga guessed that this man would have been one of those who would have been deeply affected by the great structures. The best aspect of the caves was that it had been built by the common people and monks and were not the work of professional craftsmen and architects. 'What a great tribute it is to the excellence of human perseverance and endeavour,' was Ganga's unequivocal thought. Ganga went on looking into the cases. Of course, Ganga did have the desire to explore on her own the structures but she also knew that any breaking away from the rest of the group would even make to lose her way in the caves and who would know what she might see or whom she might meet. 'Perhaps, even an ageless diminutive monk, who would in all probability be doing tapas.'

Of course, what gave Ganga the ultimate joy was visiting the cave number fifteen where she saw the Das Avatara or the ten incarnations of Lord Vishnu. She identified the most important of them, the great Lord Rama. Ganga had always cherished the image and achievements of Lord Rama. The ten incarnations of Lord Vishnu and the perfect depiction on the walls made Ganga extremely happy. The obvious inference from the structures was that religion and myths had interwoven centuries ago and it was only the ramifications that were being felt to the day. Ganga was impressed.

She went further to visit the five Jain caves. The caves were adorned with shrines, lotus flowers and surprisingly, there was even a yakshi on a lion under a mango-tree.

From Ellora, the group trudged to see the second century before Christ wonder that was Ajantha. Ajantha and Ellora had always been called and addressed together as 'Ajantha-Ellora' but as Ganga realized, Ajantha and Ellora were quite a world apart not only in terms of distance but also in terms of the ideas that the two were trying to communicate.

Ganga was dressed up in an extremely colourful orange saree and it did not at all blend with the ancient caves. Here was the new trying to compete with the old but the new was new with its freshness whereas the old had its own charm and serenity. It seemed surprising to Ganga that it needed an Englishman to discover one of the most beautiful and stunning group of caves in India. It was like an ancient secret being unraveled. Ganga felt thrilled to be a part of this voyage of discovery. She could guess as to how thrilled John Smith on a tiger hunt would felt when he and his group of British Officers discovered the thirty caves. Of course, Ganga realized that it would have probably looked odd then to know that a person from some other country was telling about your own but Ganga knew that the world was multi-cultural now where everyone needed to know about everyone else's culture to live in peace and operate in harmony.

The caves, which operated as chapels and monasteries for the monks, were an eye opener to the tourist. Ganga thought, 'In case, the monks wanted to preach Buddhism, why did they have to stay in secluded retreats, in caves, to follow their dream? They should have been out, amidst the people preaching the high ideals enunciated by the Lord Buddha. They must have enforced greater and greater contact with the people. May be they wanted somebody to come years and centuries later to discover them and to take them to the world when the world would have probably changed a lot and forgotten the tenets enunciated by the Lord Buddha live non-violence.' Ganga knew that the world was living in a world of violence and it was now than ever before that people needed to look into themselves and into the lessons taught by great leaders like the Buddha.'

The Ajantha frescoes dazzled Ganga who wanted to understand them even better. The holy monks had depicted stories from the life of the Buddha especially the Jataka tales from the lives of the Bodhisattvas. Incarnations of God were very much an important aspect of Buddhism as it was Hinduism. Ganga could easily link the Bodhisattvas with the ten incarnations of the Lord Vishnu. Ganga was especially impressed with the two Bodhisattvas, Padmapani and Avalokiteshwara. The fact, the entire caves were such that the natural light would come into the caves. Ganga admired the brilliance of the wise monks and their great artistic abilities as well as their concern for the environment. Only the natural colours of the flowers and roots had been used to paint the pictures on the walls of the Ajantha caves. What extreme beauty lay in Ajantha and Ellora!

Gujarat was a new experience for Ganga. It was full of a new and marvelous feeling which enveloped the air and brought beauty into the lives of all those who came into contact with it. Gujarat was the land of Lord Krishna as was Ayodhya, the land of Lord Rama. Several kings and emperors had prevailed over Gujarat. The Mauryas, Gupta, Pratiharas and the Chalukyas or Solankis had all woven their threads of magic in the region. Gujarat had a vibrant and colourful life with the sea breeze fighting itself into the psyche and sensibilities of the Gujaratis.

The Gujaratis and Ganga appeared to be on the same wave-length. Ganga found that the Gujaratis shared the same sense of enthusiasm for life as her. Right from the moment that Ganga got down at Valsad, Ganga was sure of the places that she would be visiting and she had already made her plan to traverse through the various places such as Surat, Banas Kantha, Vadodara, Kheda, Bhavnagar, Amreli, Junagadh, Jamnagar, Rajkot, Surendra nagar, Mahesana, Kachch and Panch Mahal.

One of the first places that Ganga visited was the Gir Sanctuary. With over one thousand and four hundred kilometers of land for the lions, Ganga imagined that the lions would be very happy. When she heard from the sanctuary authorities that steps were being taken to set up a second lion home in Madhya Pradesh, Ganga's joy knew no boundaries. Ganga was an animal lover and only animal lovers display the kind of happy reaction that Ganga did.

Ganga and a few other tourists traveled on elephants through the sanctuary and had the joy of watching the feared animals from near. Ganga noticed that the lions, whether they were sitting or lying down or sleeping, were attentive and were looking at the tourists and the elephants through the corner of their eyes and had their eyes upon them.

Gujarat was the land of Mahatma Gandhi. Mahatma Gandhi was the epitome of truth and non-violence. At Porbandhar, Ganga visited the place where Gandhi once lived. She found that the place exuded great peace and an enourmous sense of something graceful but incomprehensible.

Ganga was full of excitement in the town of Valsad. It was an important trading place for it was quite near the city of Bombay and the town of Surat. Ganga did some window-shopping in some of the shops selling cotton clothes. Afterall, Gujarat was renowned for the precision of its workers especially the precision of its jewellery makers and weavers of cloth. It was no mere coincidence that Gujarat was the land of Gandhi and Gandhi had been a great propagator of Khadi. Gandhi had always believed that it would be better to let ten thousand to work to produce something than to use fewer men and more machines if it would mean that the thousands would be thrown out of jobs. Cotton for Gujarat was like wine for France. Gujarat and its people were passionate about cotton. Their other passions were jewellery-making and designing. Yet, another passion, which brought joy to Ganga, was that the town of Valsad was India's first integrated horticultural district. Ganga ate to her heart's content. She ate all kinds of fruits and vegetables. She gave lovely tips to her waiter in the hotel where she stayed because he gave large servings of the sweet fruits and myriad vegetables.

Ganga also payed a visit to Surat. Surat had been plagued by plague years ago. When Ganga stepped into the city, she expected to see rats, cats, open drains, ill-dressed people, overflowing sewage lines and was thereby building presumptions and trying to understand the situation around her based on the assumptions. What she saw gave her a pleasant surprise. Surat was one of the cleanest places she had ever seen. It was free from rats, mice, monkeys and cats. Its roads were clean and well swept. Its highways were excellently maintained. Ganga went to the famous jewellery bazaars. Almost near the center of the city, Ganga found an entire street filled with a number of jewellery marts and gold house. Ganga learnt that the diamond business were run by individual families. Marwari and Sindhi families were extremely well-knitted with the men of the elder generation living in harmony with the members of the younger generation. In most cases, the sons, either their own or their brothers' and sister were drawn into the diamond business. Diamonds passed hands only within the family concerned and never into alien ones. Ganga didn't buy diamonds because she didn't have the money to buy them. Just looking at the diamonds through the enormous glass panes gave her immense satisfaction. Ganga thought sadly, 'Oh! I don't even have the means to buy all these lovely pieces of art.'

Then Ganga remembered something which brought a smile to her lips. After all, how could she ever forget her adventure in the hills of Arunachal Pradesh. The face of the chief of the tribals was still largely imprinted in her mind. She tried to imagine the reaction of her mother, her father and other relatives.

Madhya Pradesh was going to be Ganga's final stop in her wonderful journey. Ganga's plan was to fly back to Delhi from the place. Madhya Pradesh was what really mattered the most to Ganga. In terms of spiritual enlightenment, it was like what Bodh Gaya meant for Buddha. Ganga was to submerge in ultimate spiritual sublimity that can ever captivate man and reduce him to ashes and then recreate him to be more powerful and more perfect than he was.

'How blessed the land is and how fortunate its people are to be able to enjoy its superb and soul stirring beauties,' thought Ganga.

The state was full of minerals, especially diamonds. Some of the most famous diamonds of the world came from the state. Ganga would easily see reason. One, the place was blazingly hot and the other was that the place seemed to be the chosen place by some divine power to add it with divine gifts and gold. All kinds of minerals were able to find a place for themselves sunder the sky in the state located in central India, the inspiring iron, the magnanimous manganese, the cogent coal, the dazzling diamond, the lemony limestone and the tolerant tin. It was not without reason that the entire place was buzzing with activity. A number of industrial units had set up base in the place

The sculptures of Khajuraho though erotic did reflect an element of divinity and highest artistic temperament. Though the sculptures seemed crude and nude, Ganga knew they were extraordinary. *Sometimes, what seems crude is actually artistic... That which seems to be difficult may well be easy.* The aesthetically oriented Chandala rulers had constructed more than eighty-five temples out of which merely twenty-two had survived. Ganga was able to visit these temples and her curiosity keeps feeding itself.

Marble, the cold and white stone was abundantly available in Jaipur and as Ganga found, it had been extensively used in the construction of palaces and even homes. Of course, the rich were the ones who always enjoyed these luxuries while the poor were always uncared for. Ganga could easily guess that with so many problems in the country, the responsibility and the guilt lay only with its citizens. Ganga's heart bled several times during the journey of its owner.

The most humbling experience that Ganga had in the State was in the Narmada belt. Narmada, the river was a river, which originated the state of Maharashtra coastal belt, which was the Arabian Sea. The Arabian Sea produced two of more virgin rivers, Tapti and Narmada.

Ganga traveled through the areas affected by the Sardar Sarovar Dam. She traveled through the vast stretches of Khalgat, Dharampuri, Lakhangaon, Bollai, Awalda, Piplud and Nisarpur in an auto rickshaw owned by by a God-fearing man. Ganga talked to several people from the belt and was stunned with the kind of fierce resilience and show of unit, which was shown by the project affected families. At the time when Ganga visited the affected areas, the government was considering to raise the height of the dam. The construction of the dam had displaced tens of thousands of people. The government had done little for the people. As Ganga talked to the women and men in Nisarpur, she learnt more facts and therefore was able to develop an insight into the lives of the people who were living in worrying times.

Ganga was speaking. 'So, has not the government been able to rehabilitate you. I am sure all of you have received land as compensation for all the troubles that have chased you.'

One woman spoke up. 'No, Madam. If you are a media-person, kindly do something for us, which will help us. Everybody pretends to be doing something for us but all that is a mere sham. In a nutshell, we feel like puppets, misused and grossly manipulated. Our politicians come to meet us once in every five years to seek our vote and then they disappear like the blue moon. We are treated like dust by these so-called leaders, not that we blame them too much because we know that they too, are the product of life's fortunes and misfortunes. They too are human and make mistakes. But they must not commit injustice upon us. We have no sanitation, water, sewage, houses and land. We don't know if our voices will ever be heard. We have lost everything, madam. But we still hope that all is not lost.'

Ganga interrupted and asked, 'Land, did you say how is it possible? The officials must have given you land for cultivation.'

The woman countered, 'That is an eye-wash, Madam. In reality, we have been persecuted and tried. The land that the government had promised to give us was not given. Instead, we have been given land, which is uncultivable, the top is black and we have had to dig ten feet deep to find the cultivable land. We returned the land which had been allotted to us and which was totally uncultivable.'

Wherever Ganga went, everyone who had been displaced repeated the same story. At Awalda, a small village largely inhabited by adivasis and tribals, most of the people were poor. People poured their tales of woe to Ganga thinking that she was some kind of an angel sent from the heavens. An old man aggressively reacted to the officials who had been sent on behalf of the Government. 'You rascals, have no conscience? Have you all have no sense of justice? The Goddess of Justice has arrived and she will give you all the treatment which rightly deserve. This madam, who is standing here is a senior official from New Delhi, Central government memsahib, you get it?'

Ganga was flabbergasted. 'How quickly these ignorant people come to conclusions!' She thought.

As if reading her mind, the old man responded by whispering, 'I know that you are not an official, madam but I am just using you as a means of combating these corrupt maniacs.'

The red-faced man with a rotund tummy turned pale in fear and moved a few steps backs. Then saying some gibberish, he quickly made his way out of the situation over which, he had apparently lost control.

Ganga concurred. 'How quickly we make assumptions,' she thought. 'The illiterate are not necessarily uneducated.'

The old man later came upto her and explained as to what were the problems faced by the people. 'That man is an official of the state government. The state government is very corrupt. These officials insist on giving as cash compensation because we will be forced to pay them bribes in order to get what is due for us. It is this unreasonable red-tapism which is ruining this country. What do you think should be done to punish these corrupt rascals?'

Ganga replied bluntly, 'They should be hanged. Where there is crime, there should be punishment and greater the crime, greater should be the punishment. It is the fear of severe punishment that will prevent severe crimes from being executed.'

Many leaders, who were supporting the displaced people were already undertaking a fast, a little away from the venue. Ganga and the others who had accompanied her made their way to the venue and joined their leaders. The fasting of the people and the resoluteness of the several thousand families, who had been displaced by the raising of height of the dam and the construction of the dam sent shock waves into the official camp and slowly the displaced people started to believe that they would receive some good news which they did ultimately. Whenever and wherever, the people protest and that too, peacefully, the officials of the government are bound to notice. The experience that Ganga had in the Narmada belt was the most spiritually enlightening experience that she had had in her entire journey throughout the country. It was the resilience shown by the poor in the midst of adversity, which ultimately brought about a revolution in Ganga's mindset. Even the weak can retaliate. India is a land of unity amidst tremendous diversity. A billion people, several billion trillion ideas, loads of talent, dust, pollution, several languages, dialects, castes, religions, colours and regions provided India with the Midas touch. The beaches, the deserts, the intellectualism, the illiteracy, the mountains, the plateaus, the plains, the unimaginably strong fortresses, awesome character of the people exposes the normal tourist who comes to see the country either from another region in India or from abroad to immense emotional upheavals. 'Where else in the whole world can you find such a country, its torso, a bundle of contradictions of plenty and penury,' thought Ganga.

Finally, Ganga reached home in her dear New Delhi - a city, which seems to carry the burden of the earth much like other busy bustling large cities with huge populations like Beijing, Shangai, New York or Washington.

~ ~ ~

Ganga's mother's eyes were full of tears of joy. Her voice choked with emotion as she said, 'My dear child, you have come back, at last!' Ganga's mother began to bawl like a baby.

'And I have gained,' said Ganga.

'Oh! You have! Gold?' asked her aunt.

'Is that all, you can think of? For a minute, Ganga's mother's face darkened. 'However, 'Yes' is the answer to your question,' replied Ganga, observing the look of trepidation and sorrow on her mother's face. She knew her mother was a materialist to the core and would not be able to share much joy in her daughter gaining something more precious than gold or diamonds but of lesser materialistic relevance.

'You are kidding!'

'Think whatever you like,' said Ganga.

Ganga accompanied her mother to her mother's bed room. Her father also came with her.

'Mother, I have got something more precious than gold. I have gained wisdom and knowledge. I have realised the greatness of my motherland. I have decided what to do with my life. I want to be a teacher. I want to share everything I want to help kids, so that they can rise higher in life.' said Ganga.

*The stunned mother looked at her daughter. She realised that Ganga was no longer the docile girl that she was. She had grown and become wiser.* **Her daughter had taken charge of herself and her life and had become a fiery woman.**

'Your bag's heavy' said her mother. 'So, you have not spent the money we gave you.'

'I did spend all my money but gained much more,' said Ganga.

'What have you got in there,' asked her father.

'Open the bag,' instructed Ganga, stiffly.

Her father removed the contents of the bag: diamonds, silver, gold and jewels from far-off lands. Ganga spoke. 'I have learnt an important lesson. Life is not beautiful because it is perfect but it becomes beautiful when we make it as perfect as we can.' *Ganga was now a wiser woman.*

# Epilogue

The angularities in life take man to the higher planes of understanding. These angularities exist not only in the external world of drama but also in the inner world of thoughts and feelings. If there is virtue, there is vice. If there is goodness, then there is evil. If there is joy, there is sorrow. If there is heaven, there is a hell. What will happen if only one extreme exists in every sphere and if only the positive aspects of life remain? We are able to weigh the intangibles only by comparison but are such comparisons really necessary. Are good and evil really mutually exclusive?

Preetha Shri had been an outstanding human being. She had never surrendered herself to circumstances and had continuously overcome obstacles. She was the brightest star, who had had lived as per the dictums of her conscience, She, a fiery woman was thus, a winner.

Shree Jay was satisfied with his sense of ethics. For him, values differed with time and place. Shree Jay kept drifting like an aimless cloud of dust. He would be employed for some time at a place and whatever savings, he could make during a season would last for the next few seasons. He found work at a few more places but they invariably found out about his dishonest nature. He did not correct his faults.

Venu, the Postman had been dead for many years after he had stopped delivering letters. After the earthquake, nothing was left of his village. His land was gone, his family had disappeared, and his feelings had been crushed, all not because of the cruelty of nature but because of the callous cruelty of people!

He was a forgotten man when alive, a forgotten soul later and now, a forgotten ghost. He is still roaming in the vast expanses.

No one knows if animals other than humans go to heaven or hell and if the heaven of humans is the same as the heaven for other creations. Jup, for his part had no doubts. It is only human to doubt. Jup was quite sure for he knew that heaven was where his family was.

Jnankeshwara and Sathyavahini remained her faithful disciples and they did not want to ever leave her. They were the living examples of what Preetha had meant when she said, 'The most enduring are the most faithfully rewarded!'

Narayana and Nala lived for many years and were always happy. Nala maintained a steady and happy relationship with her friend, Preetha.

Martha led a very mundane life. She kept working at the school. She gave good marks to all her students. Her students loved her for that. She never scolded her students.

Victor, the actor par excellence was to be devoted to Preetha forever for she had brought in that spark of peace in his life, which he desperately needed it to ignite his life engine. He being an actor, living in that murky world and coming out of it unscathed was quite something. Both Victor and Preetha remained close friends. Mala was a most devoted wife.

Kasturi and her husband lived happily together.

Preetha and Vijay remained devoted to each other. The love birds were always seen together. They had two sons – Samartha and Siddhartha. Vijay became more famous, rich and sought-after and his intellectualism was hailed everywhere. Vijay and Preetha lived very happily together for many years. Preetha became more famous and richer than Vijay. **She became a legend in her own life time**.

Preetha remained a role model - a model of exemplary behaviour in very difficult circumstances. Heaven had lost its charm for her and hell, its ferocity. When the time to depart came, she was not afraid for she knew that she had led a worthy life and in the process, had made many friends and had received great fame, good-will and prosperity. She had surmounted great odds and had smiled even in the midst of adversity and poverty. She had maintained her dignity and composure even when there was little to sustain herself and her dreams.

At a ripe old age, when Bishwas and Preetha died, they went to heaven together where they met several of their friends from the earthy plains and they knew that a few others were waiting to catching up. Together, they share a lovely future. The limitation of man is that he does not know everything and sometimes it helps. As Preetha put her first step on heaven, there was Jup, timeless and ageless, swinging on the branch of a most magnificent tree....sporting the warmest smile that a simian can possibly can to welcome his beloved mistress.....

Thus, the girl from D'Salem finally was finally able to obtain, what she deserved and her life was successful. Her life is a lesson to all those, who believe that karma begins with thought and ends in action, which is a never ending vicious loop.

Now, what about Ganga? Ganga was Preetha. Preetha had got respect and wealth. Ganga too had become rich and wise.

Nothing dies in this cosmos. There are only beginnings. The only certainty of life is karma. Everything is connected by a unique compound of karma (action), dharma (virtue), sva-dharma (individual dharma), time, space etc. Maybe, there is a real God, who controls all of the above. Maybe, neither our sins nor good deeds ever leave us. Maybe all that has been given in our scriptures about God, life, death and the various truths are really true and the great truth is that Truth defines human life and not the other way round. Also, Truth remains the truth whether or not, it receives any support.

Preetha and Ganga, the evolutions of the same soul had risen on their own. Their **courage and wisdom** had earned them both **spiritual happiness and material wealth**. They were truly **the fiery women**, who lived life on their own terms – not seeking social approval to do what they wanted or what they liked. Every person who wants to succeed in life has to overcome humiliations, sufferings, sorrows and obstacles. It is only when a person overcomes his lamentations that he is able to achieve everlasting happiness and success. One needs to keep swimming against the fiery currents of life – for they are essential for our purification and resurrection!